I0537410

Necron (part 5)
Culture Clash

By Oliver Strong

ISBN: 978-0-9955188-4-1
Word Count: 27,215

Other books in this series:
Part 1-Necron: Beyond Einstein's Barrier
Part 2-Necron: Fortunate Son
Part 3-Necron: Pretend That We're Dead
Part 4-Necron: Making Amends

# Contents

# Chapter One

Darkness upon darkness, layers of space-time, fabric upon which all matter in the universe dangles as if suspended by a hidden force ... on that wine dark sea spanning stars Necron ploughs her course, sailing into view as black ships of Achaea pausing on their journey to Troy.

The sight of her hull creasing God's universal abyss did cause the hearts of every man, woman and alien to skip a few beats.

Its dark fury intended for another, yet none dared turn away lest she strike contempt into that swirling void.

An Achaean barge of dead closed on Cloud 9, a station in the Sirius A system. Sirius possessed no habitable planets but plenty of moons and asteroid belts rich in Yeonum. This station served as a place where prospectors might trade in hard earned ore and more often than not blow it on hookers, booze and splash.

As Necron's mighty Achaean boughs drew alongside, a collective gasp snatched oxygen from all directions. Chatter filled the outer ring of a giant spinning top in space. For many it was their first glance at a myth, a thing of rumour, dismissed by official media as subject for conspiracy theorists and old women with little more to do than stir up trouble.

Necron was no longer a fireside story told to children, not for the men and women of Cloud 9. Much like Homer's fabled craft, the fantasy of a desperate son, roaming wine dark seas until one day she makes harbour in your port.

Some said if not for Hitler, Nostradamus and the Necron most conspiracy theorists would have to find a proper job.

Her mighty hull slowed, coming to a relative halt as clamps secured Necron's mass in synchrony with Cloud 9. Nozzles fixed themselves to her tall blocky side, an inverted trapezium took a draught of yeonum fuel, oxygen and everything else a warship requires.

An airlock extended, latching into place, its long tube filled with nitrogen-oxygen atmosphere while security personal in formal dress assembled alongside their commander.

Curious inhabitants congregated … for the first time Cloud 9's casinos and whorehouses emptied. Citizens stood with bated breath as three men strolled an air lock tube. Two in military dress the other a cream suit with brown shoes but it wasn't their attire which caused heads to turn. Men and women usually playing black jack, getting laid or shooting up splash were transfixed by the possibility of catching a glimpse of their first zombie.

Armed security formed a barrier to supress a throng leaping above inquisitive heads. Communication devices pushed aloft unaware an EM distortion field ensured no record might make its way to crazy conspiracy theorists back home.

Sirens raised, guards forced back a swarm of bees descending upon summer's last flowers, the airlock opened, observers pushed forward, three sons of Achaea exited. The tall one clutching a swagger stick shook hands with Cloud 9's station Mayor, an honour reserved for only her most eminent visitors. The second, a grey heavy-set fellow in black and red military dress was followed by a shorter fellow in a swanky suit.

Multi-story shopping bazaars stood vacant as tombs in a graveyard while customers pursued legend on the promenade. Achaean warriors who fought terrifying demons on the edge of time graced Cloud 9, every man and woman heaved to snatch a glimpse of these fabled fighters. Just as towns folk of the ancient world might clamour in hope to see the face of Agamemnon, children scarper about to touch Achilles' cape, so the population of Cloud 9 were held in awe of modern day legends.

The scene was somewhat different aboard Necron as marines prepared for shore leave. Forty-eight hours of a little shopping between long stretches of debauchery.

Mercer tightened straps on his boots before slapping Velcro side tabs down, 'Anyone here done a cretin?'

Ting, busy spraying himself with a scent which until now had only succeeded in attracting insects, pulled a face, 'Dude, you're not gonna screw one of those lizard things?'

'I might have no choice bro.'

'What are you talking about?'

'Since they got four hands I'm thinking they're the only ones that can handle my piece,' Mercer ground his hips to the delight of his comrades, locker doors slammed in approval.

Diana was busy adjusting a wig, she slowly shook her head, permitting a sly grin escape.

'What?' demanded Mercer.

'I didn't know "piece" was code for ego,' laughter filled the air again, men of Bravo Company shared in merriment, the thought of converting six months savings into lewd gluttony pressed on each mind as the sky upon Atlas' shoulders, 'and they're called canarks.'

'Who cares?'

'Keep calling them cretins and you might get arrested for incest.'

Mercer smiled, 'I ain't letting you or nobody get to me today 'cause I'm gonna go on that station and fuck every bitch every damn way, humans, cretins and canarks baby!'

Diana waved her hand in front of her nose before looking Ting up and down.

'What now?' said Ting in a tired voice.

'You're not putting that on?'

Ting looked at his bottle of cologne then back at Diana, 'I bought this on Alpha B, it's guaranteed to send women wild with a unique mixture of pheromones and natural plant extracts acting as sexual activators.'

'The only time that moose piss ever worked you got attacked by a swarm of Alpha hornets, I guess they were female.'

'I paid ten credits for this stuff, so it better have an effect.'

'It certainly has an effect on me.'

'Really?'

'Yeh, it makes me want to throw up.'

3

Merriment filled the air again.

Ting eyed Specialist Nass, 'What the hell are you laughing at? You're wearing more pancake than a drag act.'

Billy stood in front of a mirror applying powder to his face and hands, 'This is gonna get me in mate.'

'I didn't know queer bars had a dress code on Cloud 9!'

Another round of merriment filled the locker room.

'I ain't going near no shit stabbers, I'm gonna hit the casinos mate.'

'Casinos?'

'They don't let people with implants or nanos play the tables so I'm gonna use an ECM at the door, pretend I'm not dead.'

'Dude it's a waste of time and money.'

'I got me method all worked out, I'll clean those fuckers out, hah hah hah!'

Diana struggled with her wig.

'Why don't you ever use the mirror?' asked Ruiz as he buttoned his shirt.

'I might fall in love with my reflection.'

Ruiz moved over, 'Let me help,' he adjusted a full head of hair, its blue streaks touched her shoulders, 'there.'

'How do I look?'

'The Lt's gonna be a happy man.'

'All the more for the coffee,' stated Mercer, grinding his hips to howls of approval.

Diana look disparagingly at the Corporal and stated in a coy tone, 'Do that near me again and you'll be serving decaf.'

Another round of laughter and locker slamming commenced.


Victor dressed himself in civilian clothes, jeans, shirt and jacket, he was looking forward to the next two days of leave with Diana. As he buttoned his cuffs the doorbell rang, 'Enter.'

Captain Gibson stepped inside, Victor saluted his senior, 'At ease.'

Gibson emitted a vibe similar to a lawyer delivering his fee, Victor eyed the Captain's flexi tablet in fear.

'I've got bad news Lieutenant.'

'Don't tell me, they're all out of Falafel on Cloud 9?'

'Worse,' he handed the flexi over, 'you got security duty.'

'What?'

'A small freighter leaving Cloud 9 at 0930 hours.'

'This is a joke.'

'It ain't no joke, you got an hour to get suited and booted.'

'Well how long's this gonna take?'

'Twenty four hours there, twenty four hours back and another twenty four hours regen.'

'My leave gets deferred?'

'Sorry.'

'Can't someone else do it?'

'The Colonel insisted you were given this task.'

'That son of a bitch!'

'It's a two man job, select a marine to accompany you.'

'I guess Colonel iron ass isn't up for election?'

Gibson chuckled.

Victor looked the flexi over, 'It doesn't give a cargo manifest.'

'It's classified, that's why we're being paid to watch it. Shinko's got a lab somewhere in this system, whatever that freighter's carrying it needs two Necron Marines all the way. Look on the bright side, you get five hundred tax credits for just two days work.'

'Great, I guess I'll donate to the foundation for victimised marine officers.'

On exiting Victor's cabin Gibson turned back and smiled, 'Try not to have too much fun Lieutenant.'


Victor entered the locker room, Bravo Company prepared for an indulgent weekend worthy of a Roman emperor. He scanned a mass of smiling faces, 'I have a job, 500 tax credits for 48 hours work, anyone interested?'

The room when silent, these men were long overdue shore leave and 500 credits wouldn't persuade them otherwise.

'I need one volunteer, if not I'll have to pick someone … well?'

'Why don't you go?' slipped a mumble hidden amongst a congregation of unhappy troops.

'I am smart ass but a second marine's required.'

Diana stepped forward, 'I'll do it.'

Relief crashed across the locker room as a wave hitting a sea shore.

'Thank you Specialist Zeng, our transport leaves in one hour, meet me on docking slip A-09. I want you suited and booted, no need to bring your comms equipment on this one, understood?'

Diana nodded her head, 'Understood sir.'

Vic gave her a smile before leaving the locker room. Mercer let out a great sigh, 'Phew! Dodged a motherfucking bullet there!'

Diana removed her wig, 'On the bright side I get to have some intelligent company for the next two days.'

Mercer ignored her jibe, 'Thanks Zeng.'

Billy continued to pat his face with foundation, '500 credits, after two days I'll be coming back with fifty fucking thousand credits!'

'Greedy people try to get rich quick yet are unaware they're destined for poverty,' stated Ruiz.

'You what?'

'Proverbs 28:22.'

'What the fuck you talking about?'

'The bible.'

Billy laughed as he applied makeup, 'But Jesus never played a hand with me.'


Victor exited an airlock connecting Necron to Cloud 9, he wore a mess uniform with his officer's pistol and N-13 strapped over his back. This was going to be a quiet baby sit within the system so he carried the bare minimum of two extra clips, each holding 50 rounds of depleted uranium.

Occupants of Cloud 9 hovered around the exit, their swarm had thinned yet aphids slowed on passing Necron's airlock in the hope they might discover a rich vein of sap.

Sure enough, some got lucky when Lieutenant Zellmann stepped off, his hand scanned for DNA, palm print and blood vessel grouping. He was permitted to board with automatic rifle and pistol attached to his person.

Eyes widened while lips spoke in muffles, firearms were strictly prohibited on Cloud 9. He travelled the outer promenade without a care in the world. This mythical creature emitted an aura of arrogance none possessed tenacity to challenge.

Residents stepped aside, offering strange looks, Victor felt naked beneath their scrutiny as humans and canarks alike ogled, the Emperor with no clothes.

He found it ironic a four-armed canark should regard his image so intriguing. A reptilian species bearing a vial of condensed urine around its neck thought HE was weird! 'Welcome to Sirius A,' Victor mused inside his head.

Cloud 9's outer ring was a meeting place, a transition point between the solar system and wonders within, expensive hotels, casinos, restaurants, multi-storey bazaars, a Las Vegas floating in space.

Skirting its outer ring he found the relevant docking slip. Victor approached its customs official, 'Lieutenant Zellmann,' he offered a flexi tablet.

A canark security officer sneered at his flexi, 'You are grey ghost?'

'Pardon me?'

'I speak you listen, you are one they call grey ghost?'

'That's what the Drax call us.'

'You fight Alpha B?'

'I did a tour there.'

The lizard stood on two legs, about the same height as the average human its elongated face reminded Victor of books he'd read as a child. All little boys had a fascination with dinosaurs at one point or another, this creature's head exhibited similarities to a raptor.

The canark shifted its head to the side so he might catch a better look at the Lieutenant, 'You kill Drax?'

'When I had to.'

Its four arms fidgeted, one hand held a work pad, the other tapped it, another floated close to a holstered shock stick, the other rubbed the rear of its head, something like a human rubbing his chin.

'On home world Great Prophet say grey ghost come, grey ghost fight, grey ghost win, Drax not win, Drax execute Great Prophet.'

'I'm sorry to hear that but I'm kind of in a rush.'

'Flee home world, search truth, now see, Great Prophet speak truth.'

'Listen I'd love to talk about this but there's a transport waiting for me and if I'm not on it I'm in deep trouble.'

Diana appeared behind Victor, 'How's it going Vic?'

Victor turned around, 'Fine if this cretin'll let us through!'

'Cretin? What mean?' snapped the guard.

'No offence buddy.'

Diana stepped forward and bowed her head, 'In the name of the Great Prophet we request safe conduct.'

The canark made a hissing noise, Victor assume it signified satisfaction, 'Grey ghost understand Great Prophet?'

'I have studied his work.'

The guard offered his pad which Victor met with a palm print, the pad emitted a bleeping noise, 'Permitted entry.'

Before Victor could pass the creature turned its head to look him in the eye, 'Prophet guide grey ghost.'

Victor and Diana strolled onto the docking arm, a tubular vessel attached to several slips. While walking to their slip Victor spoke, 'You've studied these cretins?'

Diana returned a matronly look, 'They're called canarks and yes I have, they're pretty interesting as a matter of fact.'

'I've got one, A cretin walks into a bar and says to the barman, I'll have a beer and a sample glass. The barman says ... are you taking the piss?' Victor cracked up at Ting's joke.

Diana shook her head, 'Just because they have trouble verbalising certain concepts doesn't make them stupid. I've read some of their texts and they're pretty deep.'

'Concepts like pissing into a bag your entire life? Don't tell me that's not retarded.'

'It's a spiritual thing, they believe it's part of their essence. When they die the body is discarded. Their distilled spirit is placed beside their ancestors.'

Victor grinned, stopped walking and fixed his eyes on Diana, 'Are you taking the piss?'

'Grow up Vic.'

He continued on his way to docking slip A-09, 'Dee, you take these cretins way too seriously.'

'There's plenty of things we do they find stupid.'

'Like what?'

'They think it's weird we worship a deity we've never seen or heard. Like someone who cashes one of those lottery cheques for a person they've never met on Titan colony.'

Victor nodded his head, 'That's pretty stupid, but God doesn't write rubber cheques.'

'You know what I mean, they worship ancestors they knew and loved, those people are enshrined in a mausoleum where their spirits reside. I think it's beautiful.'

'I got another one, why does a cretin have four hands?'

Diana refused to answer.

'Come one Dee.'

'Fine, why?' replied Diana in a tired tone

'So he can count all twenty of his brain cells!'

'Canarks have only four digits.'

Victor burst out with laughter as they approached their destination.

# Chapter Two

Awaiting their arrival at docking slip A-09, two arms folded across chest a second pair behind its back. It wore a civilian issue flight suit of canark design with metal rimmed collar so any sized helmet may be snapped quickly atop, much like a Necron flight suit.

The dark green Captain noticed Victor's interest, 'Great grandfather.'

'Sorry?' replied Victor.

'You look I tell,' he pointed to a patch on his breast depicting a canark stood between two planetoids, it laboured pushing them apart, 'Great grandfather award, display respect. You Lieutenant Zellmann?'

'That's me.'

'Captain Quetz,' he opened all four hands toward the ceiling before bowing. Diana secured her N-13 and did the same, unfolding palms as flowers searching out Spring's first sun.

Victor took Diana's lead.

Quetz offered one of his hands in a handshake, 'Welcome aboard the Coatl.'

Victor shook Quetz's cold leathery hand, 'Thank you Captain.'

Quetz's vessel was perhaps three times the length and breadth of a Blackbird yet in maintenance and arms she lacked. A civilian craft of alien design and manufacture, Victor was curious to see her inner workings.

'Come,' hissed Quetz leading them aboard as Charon on the riverbanks of the Styx, two dead warriors entering his barge for the crossing, side by side.

A short tube connected Coatl with docking slip A-09, once past the air lock Victor sniffed, then sniffed again, its innards were pretty ripe. Either the Coatl's scrubbers required an overhaul or her designers were most comfortable breathing a thicker, ammonia tinged atmosphere.

They walked into the main body. A hexagonal table surrounded by chairs, food dispensers on a wall and a couch with holo-vid player. Meals and relaxation would presumably take place here, but your guess is as good as mine when it comes to four-armed reptilians who carry their own piss concentrate wherever they go.

In the centre stood another canark, Quetz introduced him, 'Co-pilot Huat.'

Again, the ritual of bowing with palms aloft played out before shaking hands. This brown skinned lizard seemed rather nervous.

'Huat never see grey ghost.'

'Grey ghost?'

'You grey ghost.'

'Why do you call us grey ghosts?'

'Everyone hear grey ghost on home world.'

'Fine, so where are our quarters?'

Quetz led them from Coatl's starboard to port side, he motioned toward three sets of bunk beds built into the ship's hull, 'You pick.'

'Marvellous.'

Diana spoke up, 'Thank you for these accommodations and thank the Great Prophet.'

The end of Quetz's nose wrinkled up as he glared on Diana, 'Your female not speak Quetz!'

The Captain marched into the central hallway and entered the cockpit.

Diana's face turned from grey to red.

'Come, leave female!' hissed the Captain's reptilian voice from outside.

Victor smirked at Diana, 'You know, I think I'm starting to like these canarks.'

Victor entered a tight central hallway denying space that two men might stand shoulder to shoulder, 'Quetz, if you don't mind I'll bring my female, she's never seen the inside of a cockpit before.'

'Understand Lieutenant.'

Diana traced his path, red faced, her eyes burnt into Victor's back with the fury of one hundred suns.

Within Coatl's cockpit Huat stood to attention while Quetz showed off his pride and joy. Despite Spartan beginnings he'd upgraded, adding several modifications of his own.

There were four seats, two up front and two behind. Although each console had a focus the Coatl could be piloted from any one. Quetz looked down upon Diana and her red face, 'Female have problem?'

Victor took a glance at Diana, 'She's fine Captain, may we check the rear section now?'

Quetz moved between the marines and back down the hall through the centre section, opened a large bulkhead and stepped into the rear.

The engine room was an old anti matter drive, an effective source of power yet precarious.

Necron Industries had designed ships based on an anti-matter drive, firing an anti-proton and anti-matter particle at each other, their annihilation resulting in a massive release of energy.

When channelled by magnetic fields that energy is converted into thrust.

The method is sound and works well yet is far too dangerous for a military vessel. It's difficult to store anti-matter safely under normal conditions, under battle conditions it becomes a liability. One strike from an EM warhead and the magnetic field, holding your anti-matter in place, will collapse quicker than Josef Kramer's defence under judicial scrutiny, turning your warship into gamma rays and neutrons quicker than you can say "I was just following orders!"

This craft was built before humans travelled beyond their own sun, before Necron Industries stumbled upon a Drax cruiser floating in space, reverse engineered her to discovered a new safer source of fuel and superior method of travel between stars.

'Is she space worthy?' asked Victor.

'Of course.'

'Is that the cargo hold?'

'Yes.'

Victor moved to the rear, climbed down an access ladder and onto the floor of the engine room. From there he checked an electronic seal on a floor hatch.

'Has anyone been inside?'

'No.'

Victor confirmed the hatch was unopened, 'Good,' he climbed back like smoke rising to the ceiling in a public house, N-13 strapped to his back. Victor produced his flexi, 'Your destination Captain.'

Quetz took the documentation, 'Prepare cast off.'

Victor and Diana sat in the cockpit's rear stations, strapped in. Through a thin sheet of transparent carbon he witnessed a moon below. A thick atmosphere of carbon dioxide with yellow sulphuric clouds bled into the deep void of space. As if its skull had been slit centuries ago by a razor-sharp meteor. Moving on the heavenly body looked back at its nefarious work and chuckled, yellow gas forming a majestic tail, exposing the perpetrator.

Quetz spoke into a headset mic, 'This Quetz, request cast off, Captain Coatl.'

A voice replied in his ear, 'This is Cloud 9 control, you are cleared for cast off Captain.'

Quetz flicked switches on a dashboard in front of him while holding a flight stick in his other pair of hands. The ship shuddered with several load clunking sounds, it caused Victor to look about him. Diana's vision remained firmly set on Victor, her disdain, like a Spartan warrior, refused to waver.

Docking clamps released the Coatl and a small burst from manoeuvring thrusters gently pushed her away.

It took a few minutes to clear the docking arm and move to a safe distance before Quetz activated auto navigation, his ship's computer adjusted with thrusters. As the Coatl re-orientated Victor saw their destination come into view through the cockpit window.

It was still a distance away, no more than a blip on a radar sweep.

Suddenly Victor and Diana were pushed into their seats as Quetz fired main engines at full burn. Anti-matter particles met anti-protons in a glorious fireworks display. Each explosion channelled via an electromagnetic nozzle into space leaving a trial of neutrons and gama radiation.

After 2 minutes of full burn Quetz cut engines and peered at his human passengers, the canark was struck, perhaps the rumours were true?

13

'Something up?' asked Victor.

'Impressive,' hissed Quetz.

'What's that?'

'Human not endure G-force but grey ghost endure.'

'I'd really appreciate it if you stopped referring to me as a grey ghost.'

'Why?'

'I might be a bit grey but I'm not a ghost.'

His co-pilot made what Victor could only construe as a laugh.

'Did I say something funny?'

'You grey ghost, prophecy.'

'I don't understand.'

Diana released her constraints and stood up, 'I guess it beats being a cretin.'

The Captain and his co-pilot took great offence, 'Silence female!'

'What prophecy?'

The Coatl glided toward her destination as the pilot released his restraints and stood, 'Prophecy, end time, Great Prophet.'

'What did this Great Prophet say?'

'Grey ghost meet black beast, last battle.'

Victor turned to Diana, 'Do you have any idea what he's talking about?'

'They have an end time prophecy, like most religious beliefs, it says a grey ghost will meet a black beast at a specific location, fight the final battle and end the war between good and evil.'

'Like Armageddon?'

'Right, their Great Prophet made the prediction over a century ago when the Drax swarmed Tizapan, their home world. I guess he said it to give them hope since they didn't stand a chance.'

The co-pilot jumped out of his seat and hissed, 'Black beast fortunate, we fight again, we win.'

'Keep telling yourself that lizard boy and maybe one day the fairies will come in the night and make it true!'

'Tizapan female not control mouth, female beat stick!'

Diana unsecured her N-13 and fixed her stare upon the co-pilot, 'Take your best shot cretin!'

Quetz hissed at Huat in his native tongue, a jumble of strange reptilian noises neither Victor nor Diana made sense of. The co-pilot became less confrontational yet his agitation remained, like a teenage boy restrained by a parent for his own good.

'Apologies, Huat young, angry,' stated Quetz.

'I apologise for Specialist Zeng, I assure you no offence was intended,' he glared at Diana, 'isn't that right Specialist?'

Diana refused to answer.

'I said isn't that right Specialist?'

'I guess so ... permission to be excused Lieutenant.'

'Excused Specialist.'

Diana stomped into the mid-section where she might sit down and drink a coffee.

'Tell your co-pilot to watch his mouth, Specialist Zeng has a tour of duty, a bronze star and at least a dozen Drax under her belt ... she'd eat him for breakfast.'

'Eat for breakfast?' hissed Quetz.

'It's a figure of speech.'

Quetz shifted his head from side to side befuddled by the Lieutenant, 'What figure of speech?'

'You know, a metaphor.'

The leathery skinned canark glanced back at his equally puzzled co-pilot then toward Victor.

From the mid-section Diana shouted, 'They don't understand metaphors.'

Victor didn't believe it, a space faring race couldn't grasp the simple concept of a metaphor, how's that possible when they believed so fervently in prophecy?

'A metaphor is something that means something else, like when I ask someone to give me a hand, I don't want their hand literally, I'm just asking for help.'

15

Quetz made a reptilian frown, 'Why not ask help?'

'I did, it's just a figure of speech.'

'Not understand.'

'Forget it,' shouted Diana, 'the man's a cretin!'

Their voyage was but an hour old yet Diana had gone from an understanding xenophile to xenophobic Nazi in full support of the final solution. Victor did his best to mediate between bruised egos, not that he disagreed with Diana.

From Victor's point of view these canarks really were cretins, they had a backward view on almost every subject.

Women were no more than dogs to be trained and punished when acting out of turn, added to that the punishment was nearly always of a violent nature.

Adversely men had the liberty to take on a career and enjoy life to its fullest. The whole situation amused Victor, much to Diana's discontent. Her face resembled one of those old English castles. An edifice of grey stone unmoved in centuries, grim and unwelcoming to outsiders, a thick stalwart barrier, she peeked from arrow slits preparing her next volley.

Victor hung his weapon from a chair in the mid-section lounge, sat down, produced a box of cigarettes and tapped one out, 'Smoke?'

'I don't smoke,' replied Diana from across the table in an upset tone.

He put his feet up and leant back before eyeing the coffee machine, 'Would you mind getting me a coffee?'

She stood up to attention, 'Cream and sugar sir?'

Victor was oblivious as to how personally Diana had taken her previous discourse with the canarks, 'Cream thanks.'

Diana was on the edge of a thermonuclear detonation, 'Maybe Captain Quetz can serve you, sir?'

Victor lit his cigarette and blew out a plume of relaxing smoke, relaxing for now, 'What?'

'Surely serving a man coffee is far too lowly a task for a mere female, sir?'

'Dee, get a grip.'

'A grip on what sir?'

'Dee!'

'Yes sir?'

'Enough, and that's an order.'

'Yes sir!'

Diana placed a tall ceramic cup with a wide base beneath the dispenser's nozzle. She tapped a button for coffee and cream, the machine dutifully spurted it out.

She placed the cup delicately before her Lieutenant, 'Anything else sir, shiny shoe sir?'

He sighed, 'Grow up.'

'I think you're talking to the wrong species, sir.'

'We're here to guard that cargo, whatever it is, ignore them, they're cretins for God's sake.'

The co-pilot, Huat, stepped inside the lounge area, 'You speak to female?'

Victor gave himself a face palm.

'On Tizapan, female speak over male, female ...'

Diana cut him of, 'Is beaten with a stick?'

Huat became incensed. Victor sipped his coffee, provided this didn't come to blows he'd ignore both their childish ramblings.

'Your female speak!'

'She's been doing that ever since I met her.'

'You beat her?'

'Only at checkers,' said Victor with a smirk.

'Not understand.'

'Never mind, it was a joke.'

'What is joke?'

Victor rolled his eyes, 'Is it just me or do you feel a sudden drop in I.Q. every time this guy opens his mouth?'

Diana raised her brow and made a zipping motion over her lips.

'What is I.Q.?'

17

Victor took a long drag on his smoke before speaking, 'Huat, just forget it, humans and cretins have different cultures. I accept your differences you should learn to accept ours … for the sake of my own sanity.'

'Keep female silent!'

'In the name of the mother of Christ having a conversation with one of you guys is like talking to a broken record!'

'Who Christ?'

'The son of God.'

'His mother female, yes?'

'Is this a trick question or something?'

'She female?'

'Of course she was female.'

'Son of God beat mother?'

Victor's face screwed up as he spoke with an incredulous tone, 'Of course not!'

'Why?'

'Why would he?'

'All female whore, slut, stupid, male must beat.'

Diana chirped up, 'Does that include the Lieutenant's mother?'

'Yes,' hissed Huat.

Victor put down his coffee down, ominously stubbed his cigarette in the ashtray before rising from his seat like a portcullis in the Colosseum, just before hungry lions rush out to bite off Christian's heads, 'What did you just say?'

Huat looked back quizzically, 'Your mother, whore.'

Diana began to smirk, 'Lieutenant, I'm sure no offence was intended, remember it's just a cultural difference.'

Victor wasn't listening to her words, Victor faced off against a four-armed cretin, 'You've got three seconds to get on your knees and beg before I rip that forked tongue out your dirty mouth.'

'Forgive what?'

Victor grabbed Huat's throat, the co-pilot squealed like a drowning rat. Before Victor might force Huat's mouth open and tear his tongue out Quetz ran into the lounge area, 'Stop!'

Victor ignored him, the pilot pulled a pistol pointing its barrel at Victor, 'Release!'

Diana raised her N-13 toward Quetz, 'Think again lizard brain!'

Reality seemed suspended for a moment, an objective observer would have assumed this canark freighter had been boarded.

Without knowledge of events leading to the current standoff, the suggestion that within the hour ships security was attempting to rip out the co-pilot's tongue, guns drawn, would seem farfetched.

Quetz glanced toward Diana, 'You shoot, who pilot ship?'

'Then tell your co-pilot to apologise.'

'Why?'

'He called the Lieutenant's mother a whore.'

Quetz let out what must be described as a groan, a deep bass noise from its stomach exited his mouth, he then hissed in that strange alien tongue while Victor throttled Huat, his other hand forcing his jaws apart.

Huat's arms thrashed the Lieutenant to no effect, as a ship caught in a storm around the Cape he was far too weak versus such turmoil.

'Huat, he apologise, you release,' pled the Captain.

Victor let go with one mighty swing of his arm. Huat flopped to the metal floor, half dead.

The brown canark gasped for air before forcing out an apology, 'Forgive Huat, Lieutenant mother not whore.'

Quetz holstered his pistol, 'Satisfactory?'

Victor fixed his eyes on a canark cowering as a terrified animal, 'Tell him to keep his mouth shut while I'm on this ship.'

'Understand Lieutenant,' hissed Quetz.

The Captain peeled his co-pilot off the floor and into the cockpit. Victor returned to his coffee and lit another cigarette, now HE resembled the wall of a grim medieval castle.

19

Diana in comparison beamed with delight, 'Come on Vic … get a grip!'

# Chapter Three

Victor hung over his coffee, a dank fog atop the River Tyne, cigarette in hand. No longer did the thought of endless cretin jokes amuse his mind for he concentrated upon their foulness with the sincerity of a man observing the construction of gallows from a cold prison cell.

Diana tried to break the ice, 'Do you know what we're transporting?'

'No,' replied Victor in a morose key, a key similar to the thick iron rattle on his jailer's belt.

'What do you think it is?'

'I don't know.'

'How about a guess?'

'I don't know,' he took a drag on his smoke then sipped his coffee.

'Only forty six more hours to go,' huffed Diana, 'Maybe I'll go into my bunk and sharpen some razor blades.'

'You're the one always babbling about Jean-Paul Sartre, didn't he say hell is other people? If he lived now he'd say hell is four-armed dicks from a planet far, far, away.'

Diana smiled.

'I never understood your fascination with Sartre, I mean, how can you be religious and agree with that whiny French bitch?'

He was referring to the many times Sartre denounced the existence of God. It puzzled Victor how she wrestled with the two, a devotee of Sartre while respecting the holy.

'Sartre said he didn't believe in God but in the concentration camp he learned to believe in men,' her eyes glazed on recalling childhood memories, 'In China we were taught to rely on men. Then after the war my family were forced into a fallout city, a nice way of saying death camp. My faith in men became one in God.'

'I'm sorry.'

'Don't be sorry, you didn't put me there, you didn't kill a single Chinaman, you didn't fire the first nuke. And Sartre, he's just a man with an idea, I'm at liberty to agree or disagree with. I don't have to comply with everything he says to find wisdom in his words.'

'Sorry.'

'Stop saying sorry, besides I should apologise. I kinda got angry at that co-pilot.'

'Because he's an asshole.'

'Maybe, but in his culture that behaviour's the social norm.'

'No wonder they lost to the Drax. If half the population are too afraid to fight they've already beaten themselves.'

'Actually, females are less than ten percent of the population on Tizapan.'

'No wonder they're all so miserable.'

Diana grinned, 'I never thought I'd hear you say that.'

'Ah, women can make a man pretty miserable but you try commanding a company of men that haven't had tail for six months. Only then does a Lieutenant realise how vital women are in the smooth running of the Marine Corps.'

'Do I detect a veiled compliment to the female of the species?' said Diana her face glowing as a daffodil in crisp morning sun.

'It wasn't veiled at all, you remember Mercer after he was banned from every whorehouse on Alpha B. The man was so grumpy he'd have given Scrooge a run for his money.

So how come only ten percent of cretins are female?'

'Females are relegated to hatching chambers, only a small amount are required to maintain the population.'

'Relegated?'

'They do nothing other than lay eggs and nurse young. If any more than ten percent of eggs are female they're destroyed.'

'And now they're whipped and beaten by the Drax.'

From behind, the voice of Quetz opened up as he stepped into the lounge, 'Not long,' he peered downwards, 'apologies Huat.'

Victor took a drag on his cigarette, his demeanour confrontational, 'So tell me about the Drax. Did you guys beat them like you beat your women?'

'Not understand.'

'In my experience if a man gets used to an inferior opponent, when a superior one arrives he quickly falls and surrenders, like a bully in a playground that picks on little kids until one punches him on the nose.'

'Canark fight Drax long,' he pointed to his patch, a canark pushing two globes apart, 'Drax strongest, Drax win.'

Victor smirked, 'Funny, on Alpha B I've seen Drax retreat faster than an Italian in North Africa.'

'Human not defeat Drax … but grey ghost, perhaps.'

'Why'd you say that?'

'Drax defeat human same canark, same pattern, but grey ghost arrive, see footage, Drax retreat, never hear before, never see, now see true.'

'And this prophecy?'

'Great Prophet say grey ghost come.'

'How come a species that doesn't use metaphors can make sense of a prophecy?'

'Not understand.'

'Then you literally believe I'm a grey ghost?'

'You grey, you fight same Drax, yes?'

'I guess you could say that.'

'All canark say true, Drax beast, animal, use canark slaves, feed on canark blood.'

'So how come a slave gets his own ship and transports goods for humans?'

'Cannot help home world, steal old freighter, hide asteroid belt, when sun safe, travel here.'

'How'd you know where to go?'

'Quetz clever. Much talk, talk grey ghost, find sector co-ordinates, go there.'

'It's a big sector.'

'Take long time but find humans.'

'How long were you in a sleeper tube?'

'fifty years. Freighter no yeonum engine. Find system, work, find grey ghost, liberate home world.'

'Necron Industries doesn't kill Drax for free,' stated Diana.

Victor nodded his head, 'She's right, we're in a struggle with the clicks but the A Team we are not my friend.'

'What is A Team?'

Over the next few hours relations mellowed to the point lives were no longer at risk. Victor drank coffee whilst Diana inquired into Quetz's voyage to human space.

The four-armed lizard wasn't as dumb as he seemed, he'd stolen this craft from space docks, space docks his people had built in an effort to colonize their solar system and reach beyond the stars.

Unfortunately for them the first species they encountered were the Drax, on assessment canarks were considered a fine prospect for enslavement. Their physical form and mental demeanour perfect not just for hard labour but multi-tasking difficult technical jobs.

Canarks were introduced to war on a galactic scale. A species who knew little of violence were christened in the fire of the most terrible storm to befall their people.

Diana believed it was karma, not that she mentioned it, beating your mother for years ain't gonna leave you in good standing with the almighty.

Quetz described the Drax assault, catching Lieutenant Zellmann's attention. He told of impressive ships entering his system, the Great Council assumed they must have been in hyperspace for decades.

The Council failed to comprehend that Drax had broken Einstein's barrier millennia ago. While they struggled to reach nearby solar systems in under ten years Drax appeared at will where ever they pleased in five minutes.

Canarks, a naïve species, assumed the best and so Tizapan's Council greeted its visitors accordingly.

Quetz described frightening vessels, long and smooth, each body different. Not a set design but individuals of differing size and set. Much like each man's body is built along a similar frame yet no two are exactly the same. Where one is designed for hard physical labour his brother offers traits of the slender, a lean craft designed for speed and agility.

It were as God's hand constructed a fleet of angels, a miraculous vision moving toward their home world.

As vessels closed distance Tizapan's populous scrutinized them in detail, first small ribbed wings poked from the sides of each craft. Canarks concluded their purpose to be decoration since none of these vessels could enter an atmosphere. Many discussed exquisite art meticulously crafted into these angelic vessels, it excited his people igniting fervent speculation.

A few hours later and the fleet converged on Tizapan without reply to canark greetings of friendship.

Excited, canarks watched over the internet as new pictures popped up alongside speculation every other minute, too much information for a single man to keep up with. It was then Quetz saw gothic figureheads upon the fore of every Drax vessel. A demonic visage snarling into space, hunting its next quarry, a shiver jerked his spine.

Suddenly chat on the internet became wary, suspicious and before soon questions were being asked as to why they'd not replied in kind, why did they appear with such a large fleet, what sort of fire power they may be carrying and likelihood of invasion.

Before long, online conspiracy theorists, previously branded fear mongers, were proven right. Upon reaching orbit the fleet spread out and began simultaneous bombardment of every city.

After a single cycle of Tizapan shock troops landed, Drax Legions swarmed any military instillation not already replaced by a crater, canarks weren't trained to fight like this but they soon learnt.

They resisted, with space docks all around their system, canarks pulled every vessel together and fought a gorilla war, ambushing their enemy whenever a soft target left the safety of its war fleet. Piloting suicide craft disguised as captured freighters into Drax warships.

According to Quetz they pissed the clicks off pretty good, enough they sent patrols around the outer planets and asteroid belts.

Quetz said the resistance destroyed enough scout craft that patrols were cancelled. The resistance took control of the outer system, Drax commanded within, including his home world and its people.

Quetz showed his patch, 'Resistance.'

'Sounds rough.'

'Forgive Huat. Huat not fight beast.'

'If he ever wants to see the day his planet gets liberated tell him to keep his mouth shut.'

'Understand.'

'I'm sorry to hear about what happened but how are we gonna make a difference?'

'Quetz work freighter, save tax credits, pay Necron.'

'You're not gonna meet their price.'

'How much?'

'You're talking to the wrong guy, that kind of stuff's way above my pay grade brother.'

'Not understand.'

'I'm just a Lieutenant, I follow orders, I don't decide who we fight or what the bill's gonna be.'

'Who?'

'That'd be Commodore Patterson.'

'How speak to Commodore Patterson?'

'I don't know.'

'Can you speak?'

'I guess I could try but ...'

'You speak, I pay.'

'Forget it.'

'How much?' yelped Diana.

'I said forget it Specialist.'

'Make rich man, speak.'

'I'm not interested in money but I'll do what I can to bring it to the attention of the Brass.'

'Brass? What Brass?'

Victor rolled his eyes, 'Senior officers, command staff, you know?'

'Understand, thank you.'

Victor shook his head as Quetz returned to the cockpit.

'What's up?' asked Diana.

'I just thought, there is one advantage to being on a cretin ship, you don't have to buy a parrot!'

The Coatl moved through space, in the distance a pin point grew in size each hour, by the time they arrived it would be a gas giant similar to Saturn.

Victor and Diana talked about life, death and how they intended to spend time together in the future. Their conversation was interrupted by a great jolt that ran through the entire vessel shaking it as a child would shake a rattle back and forth. Victor and Diana were thrown onto the floor. The Coatl began to spin, barrel rolling, over and over, tossing the pair about like beans in a maraca.

Lights went red and a klaxon blurted what must have been an alert in a strange alien language.

Victor struggled to maintain any sense of orientation as his surroundings spun about, if ever he wondered how a hamster might feel he'd just found out as Victor's feet tried to keep up with ceiling, walls and floor spinning beneath.

Diana attempted the same, moving in the opposite direction to Coatl's roll in order to maintain a stable position.

Aboard a Blackbird it'd be un-necessary however artificial gravity on the Coatl wasn't anywhere near as efficient. The Coatl was unable to adjust gravity at such a pace to compete with its spin.

Diana tried but stumbled, her legs not as long as the Lieutenant's. Victor grabbed Diana by the hand saving her from being sucked back into a swirling Charybdis of confusion occupying every inch within the Coatl.

After thirty seconds Coatl's barrel rolls slowed to a relative stop, artificial gravity strengthened to the point they were pulled from her wall to floor. Victor led Diana by the hand inside Coatl's cockpit, before speaking he strapped her in.

'I can do it myself,' snapped Diana.

Victor moved to an opposite seat behind the co-pilot and secured his safety belts, 'Quetz, what just happened?'

'Collision.'

'With what?'

'Not certain, believe meteorite.'

'Damage?'

'Hull secure, superficial.'

'Do you have the ship under control?'

'Yes but ....,' Quetz tapped a readout then smacked it with the palm of his hand.

Victor observed a column drop from green at the top to light blue in the middle then red at the bottom before going blank, 'What was that?'

'Nothing.'

'Don't bullshit me Quetz, what just happened.'

'Oxygen breech, have auxiliary tank, not problem.'

Huat hissed to his Captain as a column beside the first began to drop, at a much slower pace, from dark green to light green, 'What's that?'

Quetz hissed to his co-pilot who leapt out his chair shooting past the seated marines, through Coatl's central section, to open her rear bulkhead.

'Quetz?'

Quetz was unwilling to say anything.

'QUETZ?'

'Huat check auxiliary tank.'

'What's up with the auxiliary tank?'

'Small leak, not problem.'

As the column slowly sank Victor's heart rate increased with equal urgency, 'What's he doing?'

'Huat drain oxygen into empty tanks.'

Over the ships communication Huat hissed and Quetz hissed back, Victor had no idea of exact content yet was vaguely aware of its subject matter. As they spoke Victor heard the release of pressure and observed the column drop quickly, he gave Quetz a look of alarm.

'Huat release oxygen into storage containers.'

The column slowed as Huat filled one tank and moved to a second. A release of oxygen filled his ears again as the column dropped like a skyscraper in demolition, an ominous crunch filled Victor's frame while a second tank filled.

Huat stored siphoned oxygen in its liquid form. Its nozzle wasn't designed for such quick operation yet Huat's extra set of hands permitted him to hold his pipe on an empty tank. Whilst some escaped in the process the majority was captured, funnelled into its new abode.

Huat managed to fill a third scuba sized tank by a quarter before the column went blank.

Quetz spoke to his co-pilot before moving from his seat to engineering, Victor and Diana followed hot on Quetz's heels.

Quetz grabbed a box of medical supplies. On reaching Huat who lay against the ship's hull, one pair of hands clasped the other, it was obvious even to Victor he was in distress.

Not having time to slip on any protection, Huat's hands and forearms were caked with liquid oxygen.

Where his brown leathery skin was covered in a frosty crust Quetz applied bandages. Huat didn't scream, perhaps his kind didn't cry out in pain or maybe his nerve endings had frozen numbing his arms with cold, Victor wasn't sure.

Diana examined the tubular tanks, similar to those used in hospitals of the past, 'How much did he get?'

'Not know,' replied Quetz.'

'Is it enough?'

Quetz finished applying Huat's bandages before helping him to his feet.

'I said is it enough?'

'Specialist!' snapped Victor.

Diana reeled herself in, 'Yes sir?'

'This man needs rest, take him to a bed.'

'Yes sir,' Diana took Huat by a pair of unaffected arms into the mid-section.

After they'd left Victor fixed his gaze on Quetz, 'Well? Is there enough?'

'Enough ... for two canark ... and maybe one human.'

Victor put his palm on his forehead, 'Wonderful, just absolutely fucking wonderful.'

Quetz screwed his face, turning his head at that odd angle canark's do so often, 'You happy?'

'No, I was being sarcastic.'

'What sarcastic?'

Victor sighed, 'Never mind.'

# Chapter Four

Coatl's crew edged her lounge table, hard stares moved between species as a barbed ping pong ball. Victor and Diana blamed the canark for their current situation. Quetz and Huat were more concerned about survival, enough oxygen existed for them, but only them.

'Why don't we turn back?' asked Victor in a stern tone.

'Cannot, thruster need oxygen, all gone,' replied Quetz while Huat nursed his bandages.

'You use the same reservoir to feed life support and thrusters?'

'Yes,' replied Quetz angling his head side to side.

'No pun intended but what cretin designed that?'

Diana gave a disparaging chuckle leaving canarks in confusion.

'Forget it, how long will it take to reach Zephyros 3?'

'Eighteen Earth hours.'

'How much oxygen do we have?'

'Course correction minimal, six hours.'

'If we use it to turn around and go back, with Cloud 9 only six hours away ...'

'Not possible,' hissed Quetz, 'slow down 2 hours, turn around use oxygen, gather speed another hour. Calculations say twelve Earth hours reach Cloud 9.'

'That's better than eighteen,' said Diana.

'Leave one hour oxygen.'

Victor lay back in his seat and sighed. As he produced a packet of cigarettes he met alarmed expressions, 'What?'

'You're not going to smoke?' stated Diana in an incredulous tone.

'Why not?'

She pulled one of those faces where a man's supposed to know what a woman's thinking but since the male of the species wasn't blessed with clairvoyance by the gods he must use his own limited means to read her mind.

31

'What do cigarettes burn?'

Upon recalling rudimentary science Victor released his packet of cigarettes onto the table along with a frustrated huff, 'Marvellous.'

'Why don't we send a distress call?' inquired Diana.

'Communications destroyed.'

'You can't send anything?'

Quetz remained quiet.

'How the hell do you guys expect to fight the Drax with this trash?'

'Coatl not trash,' hissed Huat.

'It speaks!' snapped Diana.

'Okay Dee, that's enough.'

'UUURRRHHH!'

'Do you have any atmosphere scrubbers on board?'

'Not same human scrubber.'

'How does it work?'

'Extract carbon dioxide, replenish oxygen, not process carbon dioxide. Coatl not intended for long space voyage, only inter-planet.'

'We're screwed!' stated Diana.

'Dee, I said enough,' snapped Victor, 'what about space suits, maybe someone can repair the communications array.'

'Not have space suit.'

'Why?'

'Not need before.'

'Well we need them now.'

'Purchase next time dock.'

Victor couldn't believe what he was hearing, from his perspective this entire vessel was a death trap waiting to claim her first victims. Life support hooked up to thrusters, no way to repair outer hull damage and what if there were a hull breach? These creatures didn't seem concerned by such possibilities.

'Are your scrubbers still working?'

'Yes.'

'At least we won't die of carbon dioxide poisoning. Do you have oxygen stored on the ship anywhere else?'

Huat spoke up, 'Fuel cell.'

Diana's face lit with hope.

'But cannot use.'

'Why?'

'Vanadium reflow battery low, remove oxygen, ship lose power, we freeze or atmosphere poison.'

'UUURRRHHH!'

Victor tapped his fingers on the table for a few moments then spoke, 'Alright, let's search this vessel for anything that could help. Maybe there's some spare oxygen in engineering or the cargo hold.'

'Cargo hold sealed.'

'Then unseal it.'

'Strict instruction, Quetz not break contract.'

'Quetz won't be alive in six hours if we don't find a solution soon.'

'Not true,' hissed Huat, 'enough oxygen for canark.'

Diana's eyes widened, Victor's black look kept her at bay before he turned it on Quetz and Huat. Lifting an N-13 rifle by his side Victor flicked its safety. A metal click that would've gone un-noticed under any other circumstance resonated throughout the entire ship, 'There's an old human proverb: a man should never step in what he can't scrape off.'

Huat looked at Quetz then back at Victor, 'Not understand.'

'Then let me be blunt, if anyone dies on this ship today you'll be first, understand?'

'Huat understand.'

'So, let's start being positive about this situation and find a solution.'

Diana rolled her eyes.

Victor rose from his chair, 'Quetz you're with me, I want that cargo hold open. Huat search the medical supplies. Diana you're in engineering, does everyone understand?'

The crew stood up, Quetz went to retrieve his manifest, Huat trundled into the medical section. Diana looked up at Victor, 'Positive?'

'Pessimism isn't a survival trait.'

'Sartre might disagree with that.'

'First off he's French, second he's dead!'


Victor waited as Quetz opened each of three security locks, the third refused to clear.

'Cannot open,' hissed Quetz.

'Stand aside,' stated Victor before placing his palm on the floor, 'override.'

'Identify,' came a robotic voice from a dark patch.

'First Lieutenant Zellmann serial number 02672.'

'Identification positive.'

'Unlock the cargo hold.'

'Request approved.'

The floor hatch swung open to reveal not much at all. Coatl's hold was empty bar three tubes. Victor slid down a metal ladder and approached as lights activated one at a time, unlike the Lieutenant Quetz had some trepidation.

'Something wrong?' asked Victor.

'No.'

'You look concerned.'

Victor recognised Coatl's contents as sleeper tubes, all three were upright, propped against her cargo hold wall. He approached the first, a sheet of glass covered the upper section. Its occupant obscured by a light frost. Victor wiped away a thin sheet of ice to observe a man of East Asian origin, stalky limbed wearing a pair of glasses.

Victor moved to the second, removed its frost to witness a woman of the same ancestry, short and round faced with a solid frame, somewhat similar to Diana. His eyes were immediately drawn to her chest area, underwear clasped the occupant's upper half exposing her midriff. For a moment he was transfixed until Diana's voice caught him unaware, 'Find something interesting?'

Victor broke his trance, 'Errmm yeh.'

Diana approached, took one glance at the woman in stasis then back at her fiancé, 'Was I interrupting something Lieutenant?'

'No, no, I was just examining the contents.'

'I saw what you were examining Vic.'

'Excuse me?'

Quetz was befuddled, 'Problem?'

'Oh no, I think Vic has everything IN HAND … or he soon will given half the chance!'

'Seriously, you're getting jealous over a pair of tits in a sleeper tube?'

'I'm just disappointed with the eye balls glued to them.'

'I'm a guy and I still have a pulse so yeh if I see a nice pair of tits I'm gonna stare,' he looked at the occupant of the tube then back at Diana, 'must be chilly in there.'

'Vic, you're gonna regret this.'

'Problem?' hissed Quetz.

In synchrony both Diana and Victor turned to their Captain and snapped, 'No!'

Victor moved on to the third tube, he removed sleet gathered on its outer glass, a mist impeded Victor's initial examination. For a moment Victor assumed it to be nano-mist, perhaps this was a regeneration unit? The mist slowly thinned, enough for him to examine its occupant.

Quetz screamed, a weird lizard squeal that stung Victor's ears. Coatl's Captain was rooted to the floor in terror, terror at the sight of a Drax aboard his ship. Despite its status … in stasis, alive or dead (who knew at that time?), its very sight sent waves of panic so strong Quetz's body refused to make a break for it, despite several commands to do so.

'We're transporting a click?' said Diana in a surprised tone.

Victor moved to the side of the tube, he examined a read-out beside its controls, 'Yep, and it's alive.'

Quetz squealed again, as if a pig were being roasted alive, turning over and over on a spit.

Victor and Diana peered toward the Captain, 'SHUT UP!'

They returned their attention to Coatl's cargo. The Drax occupied a stasis tube, the mist merely its preferred atmosphere, barely breathable to humans yet acceptable for a Necron Marine. Victor's nano-bots were designed to remove heavy doses of toxic carbon dioxide.

After considering the atmosphere Victor realised, he and Diana might be able to survive a carbon dioxide heavy atmosphere. Perhaps things weren't as bleak as first assumed. Victor silently pondered, for if he didn't make a move soon they'd have to kill at least one canark.

Victor removed the option of murder, he wasn't prepared to kill innocents to secure his own survival, it just wasn't his style.

'What about the others?' asked Diana.

Victor examined their tubes, 'Both are alive.'

Diana perceived a spectacled man in the first tube along with a powerful dose of de ja vu, 'I know him.'

'An old boyfriend?'

'That's Sen.'

'Sen who?'

'The butcher of Shanghai.'

'What does Shinko want with a butcher?'

'Not that kind of butcher, he did experiments on living human beings, during the war.'

'What kind of experiments.'

'Thought control, he believed we could be brought to heel via mass mind domination.'

'I take it he didn't succeed.'

'Not before thousands of civilians had been subject to his practices.'

'What did he do?'

'He inserted microchips inside his victim's brains.'

'Like they do with the disabled?'

36

'But he wasn't trying to control their body, he was trying to control their thoughts. Tens of thousands of civilians died on his operating table or were left insane, he has to die,' she raised her rifle.

Victor pushed the barrel down, 'Easy Specialist, now you don't know who he is.'

'Every Chinese knows his face.'

'I don't care what they know, I'm the commanding officer and no-one gets shot on my watch.'

'That's more than his victims got.'

'You don't know it's him for sure so just dial it down Specialist,' he scanned the hold, 'is there anything else?'

Quetz shook in terror unable to answer.

Victor stood between him and the Drax, 'Get a grip man!'

Quetz had lost control, once Quetz's eyes touched Tizapan's galactic overlord his feet rooted to the floor like old oak trees.

Victor slapped the Captain's face as he would a hysterical woman until pain overrode fear moving his attention to the marine.

Half a minute later Quetz withdrew from his malady to fix upon Victor.

'Is there anything else we can use?'

'Nothing,' trembled Quetz.

Huat heard squeals and charged into the cargo hold. At first he was shocked to see Victor holding his Captain by the lapel. Upon approaching the fracas Huat noticed three sleeper tubes, then their contents and finally a Drax.

'EEEEEEEEEEEEEEEEEEEEEEEWWWWWWWWWWEEEEEEEEEE!' squealed Huat before his legs gave way.

Quetz lurched to his co-pilot's aid while Victor looked over the sleeper tubes and stroked his chin, 'Three sleeper tubes and seven people, I guess we could double up.'

Diana pulled a face, 'UUURRRHHH, and I know who you'll be playing bunk mates with!'

Victor laughed, 'We all have to make sacrifices Specialist, I'm more than willing to do it for the Corps.'

'I got a better idea, why don't I put a bullet in nipple girl's head and we can double up in her tube?'

'Negative Specialist, we do the click and take his sleeper tube.'

'Won't work, we can't both survive its atmosphere in hyper sleep.'

'Where'd you learn that?'

'On Alpha B, our regen units were always failing or out of power. Unlike officers us grunts had to make do. A regen unit is a retooled sleeper, we can't double up and use the click's atmosphere. But if we can't remove the human occupants we can use their reserve oxygen.'

'Where?'

Diana moved to the right-hand side of one unit, flipped open its metal panel to reveal a handle that when pulled back a compartment slid out to touch her knees, 'Viola.'

The compartment contained an emergency tool box and three canisters, one of which was secured to the sleeper tube via a metal pipe.

Diana did the same for the other tube, 'We can use these spare canisters for oxygen until we reach our destination.'

'Is it enough?'

'You'll have to ask the cowardly brothers, I'm not a mathematician.'

Victor turned to Qutez and Huat still shrinking before an unconscious Drax, 'Hey, assholes, is this enough?'

They didn't reply, frozen by terror.

'Dee, get them out of here, I'll move the canisters.'

'What's wrong Vic, don't trust me with Sen and nipple girl?'

'Just do it.'


Ten minutes later the crew sat in Coatl's lounge, a couch and holo-player lay in a corner amongst a pile of debris. Her pilot and co-pilot wracked by fear of a Drax, even one in hyper sleep, fidgeted at the table. Four oxygen canisters rested before them.

'These canisters, how much longer do they give us?'

Quetz shook, his mind in crisis.

'HOW MUCH LONGER?' shouted Victor.

'Four hours,' blurted Quetz, forcing himself to swim against a tide of fear and terror.

'Four hours?' stated Victor in an incredulous tone.

'Yes.'

'But a sleeper tube can go years, decades, supporting life without the need for servicing.'

'Hyper sleep small oxygen.'

'So, we need another eight hours of oxygen.'

'We could use the sleeper tubes,' suggested Diana.

'Those tubes are already occupied.'

'For now.'

'What are you suggesting Specialist?'

'We kill Sen and nipple girl and take their places until we reach Zephyros 3.'

'I won't sanction murder.'

'Won't sanction murder? Sen murdered my people, tortured women and children ...'

'ENOUGH! I'm not murdering a man on the alleged war crimes of someone he happens to look like, is that understood Specialist?'

'YES SIR!' snapped Diana.

Victor looked at Quetz, 'What if we use this oxygen and I take the Drax's place, will there be enough for us all to make it?'

Quetz turned to Huat who made some hissing noises, he fixed his eyes back on Victor, 'Possible.'

'You're not using that Drax tube, its atmosphere might kill you,' stated Diana in a worried tone.

'But then again it might not.'

'Don't do it Vic.'

'I'm going in that tube until we reach our destination.'

'Stop being a hero Vic, it's not necessary.'

'I'm in command and I wouldn't expect any man to do what I wouldn't myself. So, let's put that click down, the quicker I get in its tube the better our chances.'

The party of four moved into Coatl's cargo hold. They'd open the click's tube, put it down and Victor would take its place. Quetz had calculated that if they conserve oxygen and open canisters one at a time they'd make it to their destination ... alive.

Upon entering Coatl's cargo hold the four were stunned to see a sleeper tube open. Its front had swung aside, its occupant, the male, emerged from hibernation.

'Shit, get that thing shut,' said Victor.

It was too late, the man had woken from a deep slumber. He was an elderly gentleman clad in white underwear, thin and of stalky stature, short hair, round face and beady eyes.

As he awoke he whispered the words, 'Am I home?'

'Shut the damned tube!'

'It's got to go through an awakening cycle before we can put him back,' stated Diana.

'How long's that gonna be?'

'Half an hour.'

'Why'd it open?'

'I guess it was on auto, after the cargo hold hatch opened.'

'Damn! Get him to medical while I finish the click.'

The old man heard Victor through a swirl of disorientation, 'NO!'

'What?'

'You cannot harm the specimen.'

'I'm sorry mister ...?'

'Joshuyo, Doctor Joshouyo.'

'Well I'm sorry Doc but we have a situation and the click's gonna have to take one for the team.'

'I do not understand.'

'We're out of oxygen and unless you get back in your tube and I take his,' he pointed his barrel at a hibernating Drax, 'we suffocate, understand?'

Without speaking Doctor Joshuyo stepped onto Coatl's cold floor, approached his sleeper tube's control panel then pressed a sequence of buttons.

'What the hell are you doing?' said Victor as he pulled the Asian stalk from its pot.

Diana examined the panel, 'He's locked the tube, we won't be able to use it for another hour … he's killed us Vic.'

# Chapter Five

'So who the hell are you and why'd your tube open?'

'I would prefer to answer those questions clothed.'

The stalky man bared his body, dressed in nothing but underpants.

'Fine, follow me.' Vic led them from cargo hold into Coatl's lounge, 'Quetz, you got something he can wear?'

Coatl's pilot disappeared then reappeared with equal haste carrying a flight suit of canark design.

The doctor slipped inside, two extra arms flopped by his side. Ill-fitting attire hung off a stalky frame as leaves on a vine, 'I suppose this will have to do.'

'Don't get too comfortable Doctor Sen,' stated Diana with a glare of revenge.

Sen fixed his eyes upon Diana, 'And who might you be?'

'Zeng, that's all you need to know.'

'How unfortunate for you,' Sen turned to Victor, 'I take it you have this Chinese dog under control Lieutenant.'

'I recommendation you play nice Doctor,' said Victor.

'Why on Earth is that?'

'We're 18 hours from our destination with only ten hours of oxygen, and that was before you woke up.'

'I do not understand.'

'Now you're awake and can't return for another hour, my previous plan of taking that Drax's place is out the window. We need to find more oxygen or someone here does the noble thing.'

'Our sleeper tubes have oxygen, it is kept …'

'We know.'

'Then the solution is obvious is it not Lieutenant?'

'No it isn't.'

'Since we are human you must execute the aliens and your dog.'

Diana's eyes widened, smoke burnt inside bringing a bloody red boil to her visage.

'Excuse me?' said Victor.

'You heard Lieutenant, they are aliens,' he pointed at two horrified canarks, 'she is sub-human, it is only logical we are to be saved.'

Quetz released his signature squeal but Victor cut him off, 'No-one's killing anyone while I'm in charge, is that understood?'

Sen moved in to examine Victor's face as if observing a piece of art, to certify its validity or discount it as a fake, 'You are weak Lieutenant.'

'Don't shove Doc, or I might just shove back.'

'Your people were weak, you remain weak to this day, unprepared to do what is necessary. It is the weak willed who disgust me more than anything Lieutenant for even those sub-human dogs had the will to repel us when your people broke into a retreat.'

Victor whispered to Sen, 'From what I hear your ubermensch ran like a bunch of frightened women at Nanchang.'

The Doctor narrowed his already narrow eyes, 'Perhaps you will do what is required when the time comes.'

Diana raised her rifle, 'I say we shoot him now and conserve as much oxygen as possible.'

'Stand down Specialist!'

Sen smirked, 'You see Lieutenant she may be a sub human dog but she has the will to do what must be done, as did I.'

'You're nothing but a butcher that killed innocent women and children.'

'I SAID STAND DOWN SPECIALIST!'

Diana lowered her rifle, 'Yes sir.'

Sen maintained his smirk, 'An obedient dog.'

Victor stood between the pair, 'I'm not sure if you want to live right now but I suggest you shut the fuck up unless you've got something helpful to say.'

Sen said nothing, his face encompassed with a silent smirk. Diana felt he was laughing inside, congratulating himself on escaping scot-free, suffering no penalty for horrendous evils compelled upon her people during the Sino war.

'What do?' asked Quetz.

'First thing's first we waste the click.'

'NO!' shouted Sen.

'Is there something I need to know Doctor?'

'That creature is an integral part of my research.'

'I'm afraid you'll have to find another.'

'I am sorry Lieutenant but that is not possible, to capture a live Drax is rare, it is more likely to win the lottery and be struck twice by lightning than gather a second sample.'

'Well that's just a crying shame.'

'That creature is property of Shinko Refineries.'

'And I give a shit why?'

'If you kill that creature you shall be disciplined Lieutenant.'

'How's Shinko gonna know … unless someone tells him?'

'I will inform Mr Shinko.'

'Should I add that to my list of reasons for putting a bullet in your head?'

'You would not do that Lieutenant, it is not in your character.'

'In that case Shinko can send me the bill.'

'That Drax is vital to research in the fight against its species.'

'Shinko'll find another.'

'Please Lieutenant!'

Victor looked Sen up and down, 'I'm sorry Doc but no dice.'

'What about the other tube, my assistant.'

'What about her?'

'Execute her instead, her tube has a proper nitrogen oxygen atmosphere.'

'You're not serious?'

'Absolutely, we must all make sacrifices for science, she would understand.'

Victor shook his head, 'You're a real piece of work.'

Sen examined Victor's uniform, now he recalled its origin, 'I thought you would understand, having sacrificed a life, a family, a career on Earth to be raised from the dead and herded about the galaxy as cattle.'

'First off you know nothing about my life. Second: I'm in charge here so what I say goes, you got that?'

Sen gave a small nod of his head, 'This is a simple supply and demand equation Lieutenant. Demand being higher than supply we must attempt to increase supply. If that is not possible, we must lower the demand before it does so of its own accord.'

'And your suggestion?'

'One of us returns to the free tube, then, both aliens or the dog must die, either is acceptable.'

Victor sighed, 'That's not acceptable.'

'It is neither acceptable nor unacceptable, it just is.'

'No-one dies today … unless you're willing to volunteer?'

Sen smirked, 'My life is far too valuable to be thrown away in lieu of aliens, a sub human or a man without the stomach to do what must be done.'

'And who made you the most valuable person aboard this ship?'

'Fate.'

'You better hope fate doesn't make you the most valuable corpse 'cause the way you're talking you're getting there fast.'

'You do surprise me, how is it you are an officer in the Necron Marine Corps yet you shy from murder?'

'Because I only kill when I have to.'

'I believe you Lieutenant. Do you believe me?'

'We're gonna find a way around this problem.'


Coatl's crew debated for the next five minutes on a strategy, bending arithmetic to fit a digestible course of action. As Colonel Rockey would point out they had it all ass backwards, arrangements are made to suit arithmetic, not the other way around.

Victor was aware of Rockey's facts, he was busying the crew before Sen's stasis tube was ready to be occupied, and who knows, a better alternative might crop up in the meantime.

Sen scanned his environment, the butcher of Shanghai formulated his own plan for survival. While others debated he slipped away as a thief in the night.

Victor only realised Sen had gone when an emergency bulkhead between Coatl's aft and mid-section closed.

Quetz rushed inside the cockpit to work on raising the bulkhead, it'd be another hour before that was possible. The canarks were confused but Victor and Diana harboured no doubt as to what'd happened.

What did confuse Victor was why, the bulkhead could be raised in an hour and anything Sen might achieve in that time would be undone in a moment.

All communication with Coatl's rear section remained fruitless, Sen refused to reply. As far as Quetz could understand Sen wasn't interfering with the ship's engines.

'We should've put a bullet in his head like I said,' stated Diana loading a round into the chamber of her N-13.

'I'm not killing anyone Dee.'

'That man's a murderer, he tortured and killed innocent people, what's your problem?'

'Hate begets hate.'

'And karma's a bitch.'

'Enough of that talk,' Victor was cut off by the sound of a massive roar, a roar he'd heard on Alpha B, 'that isn't what I think it is.'

'The click,' replied Diana.

'Damn, that crazy bastard woke it up!'

'If we're lucky he's already dead and when that bulkhead opens we can finish it.'

Quetz and Huat shook in fear.

'And you two, get your shit together or lock yourselves in the cockpit.'

The canarks glanced at one another and dashed for the cockpit, closing its door behind them.

While checking her rifle Diana whispered, 'You know if we let it kill Sen and the cretins first, there'll be enough oxygen for us.'

'Sen didn't let that thing out to kill him, he let it out to kill us.'

'How the hell's he gonna survive alone in the cargo hold with a click?'

'I guess we'll find out.'

The bulkhead lifted, tactical torches, fixed to Victor and Diana's rifles, illuminated passageways. All was quiet, they hadn't heard the click for half an hour.

On entering Coatl's cargo hold Victor expected to see Sen's guts smeared wall to wall, instead he rested by the click's open tube.

'What've you done?' asked Victor.

'What was needed Lieutenant.'

'Why aren't you dead?'

'You will have to ask my subject.'

'I've got half a mind to shoot you now.'

Sen smirked, 'I die, you die Lieutenant.'

'What's that supposed to mean?'

Sen pointed to his skull, 'I am your only hope to recover my subject.'

'Then do it now.'

'Not before the equation is balanced.'

Victor heard a roar from behind. He turned and made for the front of the ship, Diana hot on his heels.

On entering the lounge he witnessed a seven foot demon lift a squealing Huat and tear his body asunder.

Quetz lay prostrate, arms sticking up, palms to the ceiling in an act of subservience, an ornate candlestick made of leathery skin and quivering bone, trembling, wracked by an earthquake of fear and panic.

Huat's body split at its waist, the click held one half in each hand. Blood sprayed in all directions, splashing Quetz's back while he quaked in obedience. Hot alien innards slapped Coatl's cold metal floor to create a pile of steaming tripe, turning the spaceship's lounge into a makeshift alien slaughterhouse, Huat lost consciousness for the last time.

Victor took aim, the Drax didn't even look his way.

Victor fired a couple of shots, he had to be careful inside a small freighter lest a ricochet returned to sender. A single bullet hit the beast generating deep bellowing clicks, it shifted with great speed into the cockpit.

Victor moved in to finish his quarry, to his surprise Coatl's cockpit was empty. The Drax left a bloody trail to form a small puddle, a drop added to it, Victor raised his eyes to see a hole in the ceiling. Their savage interloper had used the space between outer and inner hull to travel from aft to fore then murder Huat.

'Why didn't that click kill you in the cargo hold?' demanded Victor of Doctor Sen.
'I do not know,' replied Sen as he moved to the coffee machine. The cup filled, he sipped its steamy drink, 'Ah, I haven't had a good latte in months.'
'That thing didn't kill you but it went after the pilot and co-pilot, I want to know why and I want to know now!'
'What difference does it make? The truth is it did and our oxygen supply is greater for it.'
'That'd be true if your click wasn't soaking up twice the oxygen of a canark.'
'A minor stumbling block soon to be eradicated my dear Lieutenant,' Sen set his smug gaze upon Quetz.
'We should've shot him when I said,' blurted Diana.
'That click wasn't acting like a normal click,' stated Victor.
'And how might a normal "click" act?'
'It waited around to do its killing, a click would've killed both of them and be gone before we arrived.
The way it murdered Huat wasn't right, they're cold efficient killers, that thing took its time to rip him in two, if it were human I'd say it enjoyed its victim's torment. It murdered him in the most excruciating manner possible, as if it wanted him to suffer and bring Quetz to the limits of terror before murdering him.'
'I believe you are reading far too deep into this Lieutenant.'
'I don't give a shit what you believe, I've fought more clicks than just about anyone here and I'm telling you I've never seen a click act that way.'
'An exception that proves the rule?'

48

'I'm really getting tired of your vague bullshit answers. I think you've done something to that click, you've tamed it or something because if you hadn't your guts'd be decorating that cargo hold.'

Sen smirked, a smirk which irritated Victor to no end, 'You are a man of conscience, that is what makes you weak, but you are an intelligent man, that is what made you a Lieutenant am I right?'

'Listen asshole, I'm asking the questions and you're answering, got it?'

'I understand Lieutenant.'

'I may be a man of conscience but I'm fully prepared to use whatever means necessary to get the truth out of you.'

Sen's smirk disappeared, 'Are we reduced to barbarism?'

'It seems so, now talk or I'll let Specialist Zeng here do her own little experiment on your nut sack!'

Sen's eyes widened as Diana grinned, praying the Doctor remained tight lipped.

Sen spoke in a nervous tone, 'As you wish, the creature is under my control.'

'How?'

'During the Sino war I experimented with mind control upon our enemies, I perfected brainwave projection, eventually I refined the process via implantation of tiny chips inside the brain, undetectable by most medical scanners. After we withdrew from China ...'

'You mean got your asses whipped!' snapped Diana.

Victor placed a hand on Diana's arm, 'Go on Doctor.'

'My research was used in intelligence and psy-ops. Then we met the Drax, I and my work was appropriated by Shinko Refineries. I assume he desires to implant moles and saboteurs within the Drax military and political structure, to gather information and weaken our enemy.'

'So how do you control it?'

Sen pointed to his skull, 'The master chip is implanted in my head.'

'Then order it here so we can dispose of it.'

Sen shook his head, 'Not until I have eliminated my competition, Lieutenant.'

'Competition for what?'

'Life.'

'Now that you're a threat, what's stopping me from killing you and doing the click afterwards?'

'Because I control it, after I have eliminated the unworthy I shall bring the subject before you for execution, Lieutenant.'

Diana sneered, 'Don't tell me you believe his fairy tale?'

'Of course not, he'll kill us all so his subject can survive, isn't that right Doctor?'

'What difference does it make Lieutenant, you are a man of high moral character, you do not have it in you to do what is required for if you did I would not be forced to do it for you.'

'I'm not a violent man Doctor but if shoved I'm gonna shove back, do you understand?'

Sen made that smug grin only to be taken surprise by a right uppercut from Victor, knocking him out cold on the lounge floor. Sen flopped on his back and as he did a roar reverberated through the ship sending fear to the bones of every crew member.

'I say we finish him now.'

'No, we might need him.'

'For what?'

'I don't know but I don't want to kill anyone unless necessary.'

'Vic, he deserves to die!'

'I've never seen you like this Dee.'

'Like what?'

'Blood thirsty.'

'If he'd done to your people what he did to mine you'd be blood thirsty too.'

'Probably … but he didn't and I'm the officer in charge so he's not going to be executed for alleged crimes decades ago.'

'Alleged crimes?' she said in an incredulous tone, 'he just admitted it to your face!'

'He said he did some experiments in mind control during the war.'

'Isn't that a war crime?'

'Look this isn't the Hague and I'm not a judge so let's forget about the past and focus on the here and now. We've a click on the loose, an ever-decreasing oxygen supply, with only one sleeper tube set up for human habitation.'

There was a roar and a scream from the cargo hold.

'I got point!' shouted Victor as he raised his weapon and moved cautiously into the hold.

Diana watched Victor's back as Quetz pulled his pistol sticking with the party. They entered the cargo hold to find no Drax but a dying assistant. Her chest bled from five puncture wounds made by the creature's finger nails. Her throat bulged where the animal had bitten in, searching for sustenance.

Diana scanned the room hunting her prey yet it'd made an escape through a crack in the floor, broken apart under Sen's watch. She allowed herself to examine the dying body of Sen's assistant, apart from red spots on her chest and neck she was pale.

Diana smiled, 'Those nipples look pretty drained.'

'You're a real comedian you know that Dee?'

'It's called a dead pan delivery, I've been working on it for some time.'

'What dead pan?' hissed Quetz, finally able to push a sentence between terrified lips.

Victor and Diana looked at Quetz, in synchrony they snapped, 'Oh shut up!'

# Chapter Six

Sen awoke from imposed slumber, his vison settled from a blizzard of chaos to focus on Lieutenant Zellmann sipping a black coffee, relaxing in his seat.

'He's awake,' said Specialist Zeng.

Sen turned left yet his movement was constrained. Sen was strapped to his chair with electrical tape, arms, legs, waist and chest tapped to its frame, the doctor was outraged, 'What have you done?'

'You're smart, work it out,' stated Diana.

The fact he couldn't see an armed Chinese soldier made the doctor nervous. His situation generated anxiety for he'd spent his life in control. Sen used and abused human beings ... subjects as he referred to them. While his "subjects" were restrained, their minds kicked and screamed in terror, he the master, they slave, now the tables had turned.

'What is the meaning of this Lieutenant?'

'I don't trust you Doctor Sen.'

'Yet you trust that Chinese dog?'

Victor placed his cup on the table and gave a hard stare, 'The question is do you trust me?'

Sen sneered, 'Do not waste our time attempting to frighten me. You have a weakness Lieutenant, you possess a conscience.'

'And I guess you're gonna take advantage of my weakness in order to make it back alive?'

'Why ask questions to which you know the answers?'

'You sound pretty cocky for a guy strapped to a chair with no buddies and a click on the loose.'

'But I control the beast and your survival necessitates I remain conscious my dear Lieutenant.'

'I did fine just now, though I can't say the same for your assistant.'

Colour drained from Sen's face, 'Nori?'

'Was that her name?'

'What have you done with Nori?'

'I haven't done a thing, the click sucked her dry.'

Sen's face began to contort, Victor assumed it to be a nervous twitch.

'I'm sorry,' said Victor.

'Sorry?'

'Yes.'

'Is that all you have to say?'

'What do you want me to say?'

'She was not just my assistant, she was my DAUGHTER!'

Sen thrashed struggling to escape his bonds, his efforts were fruitless. He tugged one way then another as a sailor in a storm. Sen let out a cry of pain, at the same time a roar could be heard from deep within Coatl's bowels.

'Doctor Sen, CALM DOWN!'

The Japanese scientist continued to wail, he shrieked so loud Victor got up and slapped his face.

After a few minutes of pouring his soul into life's vessel of regret Sen's excess energy had expired, he began to weep for his child.

'Karma's a bitch,' snapped Diana.

'SILENCE THAT CHINESE DOG!' bellowed Sen.

'You were okay with wasting your assistant an hour ago.'

'A ploy to conceal my weakness, it was obvious the Lieutenant would never sanction her execution.'

'At least she had a quick death.'

'SHE WAS AN INNOCENT!'

'SO WERE THOSE PEOPLE YOU MURDERED DURING THE WAR!'

'They were nothing, THEY WERE SUB-HUMANS!'

'Okay, give it rest you two. I don't need another lecture on the Sino-war, what I need is a solution. We're down one canark but we're up one sleeper tube, Quetz, how does that put us?'

'Use sleepers, I pilot alone, can do. Not air more than one.'

'Okay, Doctor I want you to bring the click to us so we can put it down.'

Sen was a shattered man, his smug grin dismissed in favour of hopelessness, 'I would have given my life for her, she was my weakness but now, now I have no weakness, I have nothing to lose.'

'I need the click to come here.'

'If I were to comply you would kill my subject then shoot me ... my daughter would be lost for nothing.'

'Your daughter was lost because you set that thing free,' snapped Diana.

'SILENCE YOUR DOG!'

'Look at it this way, if you don't bring it here you're no use to me. In fact, you're a liability, because all the time you're alive you're wasting oxygen while alerting that thing to my plans.'

'Then kill me Lieutenant, I have nothing to live for now Nori is dead.'

Victor took a deep breath before reaching for his pack of cigarettes.

'Hey Vic!' snapped Diana.

'Dee, I need to think.'

'Those things burn oxygen.'

'Just one?'

Diana pressed her lips together in a dissatisfied grimace, 'Fine.'

Victor pulled a camel out its packet igniting the foot with his green yeonum lighter. He drew in smoke, as a thick nicotine cloud hit his lungs calm chased tension from his body. He contemplated the situation as a Zen Buddhist, meditating on the expanse of human thought within the universe, atop a mountain in still morning air.

'Sen, I have a plan.'

'Save your talk Lieutenant, nothing you say could coerce my thoughts.'

'You said you'd do anything for Nori?'

'I did.'

'Would you die for her?'

'Without a doubt.'

'Then I've got a plan, but we need to move fast.'

Quetz removed a vial of condensed urine from Huat's neck, his body to be discarded while his spiritual essence preserved.

Quetz couldn't do it now but one day he'd return Huat to his ancestral tomb on Tizapan.

Quetz had dealt with the loss of his shipmate. The terror of Huat's violent departure faded as an old oil painting of a savage battle on the plains of Troy. Detail worn away, blood spray no longer held its former vibrant tone. Trojan innards hanging from Achilles' spear blurred with age, aspects no longer sharp and sophisticated but dull and crude.

Quetz went on his knees and made a prayer to the universe, he prayed for retribution, for justice, simple things all sentient beings desire.

'What is he doing?' asked Sen.

'He's praying,' replied Diana.

'For what?'

'That his enemy will pay for violating his countryman.'

Sen fixed his gaze on Diana, 'Do you desire revenge?'

'I do.'

'You may yet have your wish.'

Quetz stop hissing and rose. He attached Huat's spirit to one of many necklace's rungs, he was now its guardian, 'Lieutenant, I ready.'

'You and Dee go to the cargo hold, get a piece of metal plating from stores, I'll watch the Doctor.'

'Understand,' Quetz exited followed by Diana.

Both marines carried rifles, loaded and ready to go despite Sen's assurance the beast would not attack again.

'Really Lieutenant, I could order my subject to space itself.'

'How do I know it can't survive in a vacuum long enough to damage this ship?'

'You have my word.'

Victor lit another cigarette, 'Words are worth little insurance ... even from the cleanest of mouths.'

'Then why do I trust your word?'

He inhaled aromatic smoke before exhaling a puff, 'Because you're tied to a chair and I'll waste you if you don't?'

'I can see you are a man of your word Lieutenant. Your conscience would not permit you to break it.'

'If you go through life breaking your word people stop believing you, then they start ignoring you and before long you're no different than a ghost. Traveling existence un-noticed, a faded sketch that might once have been a great work, instead the artist chose to discard it, deeming it unworthy of his time, his effort, or even cost of paint to fill in the spaces.'

'An interesting philosophy, I see why you wear that uniform and carry two stars on your shoulder.'

Victor took a sip of coffee before drawing thick smoke again.

'You are a leader my dear Lieutenant, men will follow and die for people such as you.'

'That's their job.'

'Is it? I read reports on Guangzhou, men broke, opposed their leaders and fled for safety. I saw it again at Shanghai, soldiers trained to follow lay down arms shaking in fear as children shivering in the night, their leaders ignored.'

'That wasn't my war.'

'But this is, this war against the Drax is your war Lieutenant and it is men like you who are required. For even that Chinese dog obeys despite faced by the thing she hates most in the universe.'

'Specialist Zeng obeys orders, she's a marine.'

Sen's smug visage returned, 'You do not understand the animosity between us Lieutenant, it goes back not just to the Sino-war but centuries of hatred and murder. She would have killed me on sight had you not been present. At first I was surprised, but now I understand, you are an exceptional man.'

Victor replied in a sardonic tone, 'Thanks, that really means a lot to me.'

'And modest.'

'Please, you sound like my mother.'

Sen looked down, 'My mother was ashamed of me.'

'What happened, you gave a Chinaman a blowjob?'

Sen made a wry smile, 'I used my education for evil, or so she said. Instead of healing sick I ailed healthy. I told her our people needed help to fight the sub-human horde lest they overrun our homeland, but she remained adamant until her death.'

'Well ain't that just a crying shame.'

'Do not mock me Lieutenant.'

'Yeh well don't expect any sympathy either. What you did was evil, on that point I agree with Dee. You deserve to be punished for those crimes, and whatever you say Dee isn't sub-human ... I can't say the same about you.'

'And how do you make the distinction between who is human and sub-human Lieutenant?'

'I base it on action, not breeding or features, and based on your actions I'd be ashamed to call you a member of the human race let alone my son.'

'Conscience, honour, modesty and now conviction, you are a man of great virtue Lieutenant. Tell me, have you done anything you are ashamed of?'

'Haven't we all?'

'What have you done that you are ashamed of Lieutenant?'

'I've lied to get what I want.'

Sen sneered, 'Come Lieutenant, what are your failings?'

'I've killed people, innocent people, on occasion.'

'Why?'

'Because I had to.'

'Why?'

'Why what?'

'Why did you have to?'

'Because they would've killed me, they would've killed my platoon, hurt the ones I love.'

'And for the same reason I joined the Neuro-warfare division of the Japanese military, because they hurt the ones I love.'

'And now the ones you love hate you for it.'

'Yes, which is why I'm helping you, you are a man of your word and she is the only person alive in this universe who still loves and accepts me for who I am. When I look into her eyes I do not see the butcher of Shanghai staring back, I see a loving father and I will do anything for her Lieutenant.'

'Then you better pray this works Doc, or we're all going to hell.'


Diana and Quetz returned, Quetz carried a large sheet of thin metal in his arms while Diana lugged two ruck sacks, one full of wiring slung over her back and a blow torch in the other.

'We got everything you asked for,' stated Dee placing a small handheld torch on the table.

Victor unsecured his rifle and using the butt tapped Coatl's lounge ceiling until a hollow sound met his ears, 'Here, move the table back and place the sheet beneath.'

Quetz transported a steel sheet, about half the height of a man and twice his girth, placing it where Victor directed.

Diana moved the table and chairs to the wall, Sen observed from his restraints.

Victor opened a ruck sack to uncover reels of copper and silver wire, 'Okay, you think there's enough?'

Quetz bobbed his head from side to side as canarks do, 'Enough.'

'Let's do this.'

Quetz took the blow torch in one hand while others arranged wires, a multitude of limbs permitted speedy work, Victor was quite astonished to see a canark in action. When focused it was obvious a canark could achieve his goal quicker than any human. It dawned as to why Drax valued their enslavement, with these creatures working in your factories and space docks your fleet became all that more formidable.

Sen narrowed his eyes on the reptilian, 'It seems I may have underestimated these aliens.'

Diana shone her gaze upon the captive, 'A genetic flaw most Japanese carry.'

Sen smirked, 'I apologise for my previous words Specialist Zeng.'

Diana's eyes widened in surprise.

'I misjudged you and your abilities, not due to a genetic flaw but a long held prejudice both our peoples have carried for centuries.'

'You'll not get absolution from me.'

'I only wish to say I was wrong concerning you, not your race.'

Victor lit up another cigarette, 'That kinda blows apart your whole theory on the Chinese though, doesn't it?'

'In what sense Lieutenant?'

'Well, if one isn't a sub-human maybe there's another that isn't and more after that?'

'An interesting theory Lieutenant but I have spent far too many years and invested far too much energy in proving otherwise.'

'Out of curiosity, what's your standard for being human? What would you accept before you'd admit her people aren't sub-human?'

Sen's expression became one of a man caught off guard. A boxer who'd left an opening in his defence only for his opponent to take advantage of that mistake. Before the pugilist might realise, he's swimming in his own mind after a strike from nowhere has sent him to the canvas. He looks up to see the referee counting him out while the ceiling swirls about as a flock of buzzards over a carcass.

'Cat got your tongue?'

'I errrmmm, I do not know.'

'That doesn't sound very scientific to me.'

'If Chinese were not sub-human dogs, why would we be at war with them?'

'You tell me Doc.'

'Your question is irrelevant Lieutenant.'

Victor blew a puff of smoke in Sen's face, 'Humour me.'

'China has always opposed us, it is what they live for, to make my homeland theirs and my people their slaves.'

'Funny, all the Chinese I know say exactly the same about your country.'

'They are liars.'

Diana's visage moved to one of anger yet her hot fire was supressed by Victor's cold expression.

'Even if what you say is true you still haven't answered my question Doctor.'

'Your question is irrelevant, they are sub-human animals, that is all.'

'Except Specialist Zeng?'

'She has certain qualities I have not witnessed in her race before.'

'Since the only Chinese you encountered previously were strapped to an examination table and fearful for their lives that's not a surprise, is it?'

'And now I am in their position, but do you see me act as an animal, unable to control my emotions?'

'No, I see you for the cold calculating bastard you are, but you keep avoiding the question.'

'Very well, I shall answer your question Lieutenant. The standard for humanity is one's ability to sacrifice his life to save another.'

'Then you've got it all wrong Doctor.'

'Why is that?'

'I can tell you from experience there are plenty of Chinese prepared to risk their lives to save others.'

'That is different, I mean outside of a military, without obligation or reward, to sacrifice for another life with no-one ever knowing, that is the standard of humanity.'

'Like I said you've got it all wrong.'

Sen remained obstinate, 'Your words are irrelevant.'

'Fine, let's get this show on the road. Quetz, how's it coming along?'

'Finish plate, must connect ship power.'

'How long?'

'Do properly, 30 minutes.'

'You need help?'

'Quetz do alone.'

'I spent years working on my creation,' mourned Sen.

'My heart bleeds for you,' stated Victor in a sardonic tone.

'It would have tipped the balance against the Drax.'

'How's that exactly?' said Victor before he drew down on a smoke.

'Spies, sleeper cells, saboteurs, it would have undermined them from within, crumbled their power structure, illuminated their weakness.'

'I'm sure someone will carry on your work.'

'There is but one other with the knowledge, ability and will … my daughter.'

'So nipple girl really is your daughter?' yelped Diana.

'Nipple girl?' stated Sen in wonder.

'It's a long story,' replied Victor in an embarrassed tone.

'I have half an hour to spare Lieutenant.'

'Long story short, sleeper tubes are cold inside, your daughter had …'

Diana cut in to finish the sentence Victor couldn't, 'He means she had a nice rack and a tight bra.'

'Dee!'

'Is there something I missed Lieutenant?'

Sen's face screwed up, 'You were ogling my daughter's breasts?'

'Hey I wouldn't call it ogling.'

'More like drooling with intent,' snapped Diana.

Sen spoke in a disparaging tone, 'Lieutenant, I find your behaviour most reprehensible.'

'Jesus Christ, will someone give me a break?'

'Don't tempt me Vic!'

Victor turned to Diana and spoke in an incredulous tone, 'Excuse me?'

'You heard me.'

'This guy,' he pointed at Sen, 'butchers thousands of people and you're ragging on me for staring at another woman?'

'For mentally undressing a woman in suspended animation while slobbering down your chin like a mental patient.'

'Come on Dee, I'm a guy what do you expect?'

'I expect some self-control around other women.'

Dr Sen raised his brow, 'That's quite an impressive young lady you have there.'

'Aren't I the lucky one!'

61

# Chapter Seven

The scene was set, survivors lined the East wall. Hatches shut, Coatl's lounge area closed off with no method of escape, at least for them.

On the room's Westside a steel square spanned the floor. Insulated wires trailed from a power point in the wall, charged streams converging on an electric lake. The plan poetically simple, Sen lures his subject in for another kill, it descends from between ceiling and hull to an electric reception.

The pad would either fry or disable the creature. Victor was uncertain which, yet Quetz assured there'd be enough juice to transform any Drax into an omelette.

Victor let his cigarette fall on the floor before snuffing out its life via regulation boot, 'Let's do this.'

Sen concentrated, eyes shut in deep thought. Diana was torn where to aim her weapon. As far as she was concerned Sen was just as likely to stab them in the back and attempt another murder. Victor was naïve, for if he possessed a fraction of her experience he'd have shot Sen long ago.

Quetz could barely stand, clutching an old pistol, its barrel shook all about in terror, teeth chattering like a man in the depths of winter, unable to control himself. In another hand he carried a remote, when the Drax touched down he'd hit a switch to concoct a fry up.

'You okay?' asked Victor.

'Quetz do job.'

The room went silent, after a few minutes noise could be detected, traversing pipes and rigging above, something was moving. Coatl's ceiling creaked at certain points, Diana raised her barrel, Victor pushed it down.

Zellmann refused to fire until they had a definite target, the difference between a trained marine and scared civilian. They were inside a freighter, room was tight. Fire on auto at non-targets and they were just as likely to kill themselves with ricochets.

The alien melody passed, Diana and Quetz gave each other quizzical looks.

'Eyes on target,' whispered Victor awaiting his foe's appearance any second. Another minute passed without sound.

'Sen, what's happening?' whispered Victor.

The stalky man, taped to a chair, replied, 'Do not disturb my concentration Lieutenant.'

'Where is it?'

'It is here …'

With that the cockpit hatch smashed off its hinges and into the lounge. Through the wall a Drax burst brandishing titanium nails, clicks saturated ear drums with terror as a vessel fills with blood red wine at a banquet. It's gothic visage, somewhere between a vile hellion and vampire bat frowned with hatred and spite. It's body, naked to the universe, covered in whispy dark fur, muscles flexed hard, its mere presence enough to terrify a grown man into immediate submission … but Victor was no ordinary man.

Victor observed the hatch laying atop their trap, 'Time for plan B.'

'Plan B?' yelped Quetz as the Drax ripped wires from Coatl's wall.

'Kill it before it kills us!'

Quetz was frozen in terror, he couldn't even hit the switch of his remote. Sen began to panic, no longer in control of his subject, between his will and that of the beast a grey area existed. Sen's subject had monitored Victor's scheme, devised plans accordingly, and so the battle began.

Sen restricted to a chair while his subject roared, the creature's anger focused upon him. His subject desired an end to its suffering and to do that its master must die.

'LIEUTENANT, KILL IT QUICKLY!' screamed Sen as a beady eyed monster opened saliva filled jaws and bellowed.

'Careful shots,' said Victor as he and Diana fired on single.

*BANG* take aim *BANG* take aim *BANG*

The Drax charged for Sen despite receiving several bullets, a satanic beast persisting a flurry of silver bullets, individually purposed with supreme will, depleted uranium but a minor drag on its goal.

*BANG* take aim *BANG* take aim *BANG*

Sen screamed like a girl as the Drax approached striking distance, he struggled rocking back and forth on his chair as a madman in an asylum, strapped down for his own good.

The Drax entered striking distance, Victor fired point blank. The greater part of its momentum had been mitigated by N-13 rounds causing it to stumble.

Victor took aim, dead on the creature's skull and said in a deep determined voice, 'Hasta la vista, BABY!'

The Drax turned to stare him dead in the eye, *BANG* it was frozen for a second as brains exploded from its rear to cover Sen in a sticky goo.

The vile hellion collapsed, yielding its life to the Erinyes, the furies of death. Victor put two more rounds in for good measure, a Drax is never too dead for another round.

Doctor Sen now wracked in terror, Drax brains covered his face and canark flight suit, this was the first time he'd glared into the abyss of his own mortality.

Diana checked life signs to confirm the beast's death. As she rose Diana betrayed a quizzical expression, 'I didn't know you spoke Spanish.'

Victor hung N-13 over his shoulder while searching for a smoke to quiet his pounding heart, 'I got it from an old movie.'

'What's it called?'

'It's one of those action movies Nass is always watching.'

'Oh you mean the testosterone fuelled egomaniac genre?'

'Hey there's nothing wrong with those movies.'

'He tried to get me to watch one,' she said in a snotty tone.

'Which one?'

'I don't know, some guy who couldn't act to save his life's daughter's kidnapped so he goes on a macho killing spree.'

'Ah, you mean Commando, that's an awesome movie!'

'I guess you need a penis to fully appreciate it,' quipped Diana.

'Ahem!'

Diana and Victor turned to observe Sen lying on the floor strapped to his asylum chair, Drax brain sliding down his face. The creature's blown out skull lay in his crotch area while alien brain stem dispersed puffs of steam.

Victor lit his smoke and took a drag before commenting, 'That would make a good movie.'

'You think there's a big market for Drax necro porno?' laughed Diana.

Sen's chair had been set right causing slime to move down instead of across his face, 'Do you mind?'

'Mind what?'

'Now my subject is destroyed perhaps you might release me?'

Victor smiled, 'Hey Dee do you remember this,' Victor quoted from his movie, 'What did you do with Sully?' he then replied to himself in that deep dead pan tone, 'I let him go!'

Diana shook her head whilst Victor chortled, the release of tension caused a relapse into merriment. Despite the fact she didn't share his taste in humour Diana allowed a pinch of a smile to escape the grasp of pursed lips.

'EXCUSE ME LIEUTENANT!' snapped Sen.

Victor fixed his eyes on a sorry sight restrained by electrical tape and burst out laughing in the doctor's face.

'MR ZELLMANN CONTROL YOURSELF!'

'That's easy for you to say,' laughed Victor.

'Will someone remove my bonds?'

Victor recovered from his moment of humour, 'Quetz cut him out.'

Quetz stood with back pressed against the lounge wall, he grasped two vials of urine dangling off his neck whilst hissing a religious chant.

'Quetz!'

The reptilian's eyes remained fixed on the Drax while he mumble to whatever ancestors he believed in.

'QUETZ!'

The Captain snapped out of it shifting his gaze to Zellmann.

'It's dead, cut Sen free.'

66

Quetz shook his head, 'Cannot move.'

'Why?'

'Black beast, spirit.'

'Dee, move the body.'

'Gee thanks Vic!'

Diana dragged a seven foot corpse to the other end of the room, a skid mark of black blood and cerebral fluid inked its path.

Quetz stepped carefully over the smear before slicing Sen's bonds.

'Are you sure you want to do this Vic?'

'He kept his word, so I'm keeping mine.'

Diana dumped the alien carcass and moved to her boyfriend's side, 'I'd waste him now, it's more than he deserves.'

Quetz finished cutting Sen free.

'Could someone get me a towel?'

'Get it yourself,' sneered Diana.

'As you wish,' Sen stepped over his specimen's corpse into the bathroom.

'Be quick, you don't want me coming after you.'

'As you desire Miss Zeng.'

Sen disappeared into the bathroom and Diana turned to Victor, relaxing his mind and body with tobacco, 'Why don't we do him now?'

'We have a deal.'

'I know you gave your word Vic but this guy's a piece of shit, if you went back on it no-one would care.'

Victor took a long drag on his stick before replying, 'I would.'

'This is one occasion I agree with Colonel iron pants, sometimes you gotta remember you're in the Marine Corps not some UN mission of mercy.'

'So on occasion I have to be a cold hearted two faced bastard?'

'Well yeh.'

'Tell me Dee when are those occasions?'

'Sometimes it's necessary.'

'You mean, when it's expedient?'

'I didn't say that.'

'Then answer my question, when do you think it's necessary to break my word or go back on my promise?'

'When our survival's at stake.'

'Sen has agreed to sacrifice himself already.'

'I'm not talking about that and you know it.'

'You'll be safe,' Victor smiled on the woman he loved. Her face, though grey, in his eyes and mind shone as a white lotus blossom in bright Spring sun.

'I'm talking about you. You're risking your life when you don't have to. Vic, I don't want to lose you, if I did I couldn't carry on.'

'Come on Dee, you'd do fine, you're the best Communication Specialist in the Corps.'

'Don't patronise me! You think I enjoy being a marine? Getting my ass shot off by crazies or waking up each cycle with thirty horny guys who talk about nothing but sex and sports!'

Victor took a drag on his smoke, 'I thought those were plusses.'

'Don't try to laugh it off Vic. I'm here because I love you, not for the Corps, not for humanity, not to defeat the Drax and not to see you risk your life on a promise to a butcher like Sen.'

Sen appeared from the bathroom, his hands and face cleaned, 'You waste your breath Miss Zeng. Your boyfriend is a man of his word, to break it would be to betray himself, it is not in his nature to do so.'

'We're not all as virtuous as Vic.'

'You could not betray Mr Zellmann anymore than he would betray me, that is not in your nature.'

'You really are an annoying little asshole, you know that?'

'Then you must be thankful for I shall be leaving you soon.'

'Not soon enough.'

'The only question that remains is how should I pass from this life to the next, do you have any ideas Miss Zeng?'

'A few, but they are all bloody, violent and excruciatingly painful.'

Sen grinned as he sat at the table, 'Coffee please.'

'Get your own.'

The doctor got up to extract a cup from its recess in the wall. He observed latte pour from a metal tap attached to a silver and black unit bought on Cloud 9. Canarks enjoyed their coffee as much as humans, a universal drink, Victor wondered for a moment if Drax indulged in it.

'I was thinking of poison, that is if we have any.'

Victor's eyes moved to Quetz, still mumbling chants to ancestors while grasping vials, 'Quetz, you got anything Doctor Sen could put in his coffee, to poison him?'

'Morphine in medical cabinet.'

'Get it. The Doctor can pass away quietly in his sleep.'


Quetz tried to control his shaking as he fumbled through Coatl's medical supplies, stored in adjoining sleeping quarters. Victor lit another cigarette, Sen addressed his jail keeper, 'Could I have a cigarette Lieutenant?'

'Sure, I didn't know you smoked.'

'I gave up many years ago, when my wife was pregnant.'

'Is she still on Earth?'

'Shem is no longer of this Earth or universe. Shortly after giving birth she died in a rocket attack on Shanghai. I insisted she remain in Japan but Shem was a stubborn woman.'

Diana let out a loud exhale.

Sen took his cigarette, spluttering on his first drag of tobacco in decades, 'Until that point I had hurt no-one, I was a doctor not a monster. Everything changed that day, after her burial in Japan I left my job as a neuro-biologist and joined the military.'

'What did you do before your wife was killed?' asked Victor.

'I had a minor position working on mental trauma patients,' his gaze moved to Diana, he took another puff, 'Japanese and Chinese received equal treatment. We worked for a university with the United Nations healing war victims, my wife was a universalist, she believed we are all the same within, no soul more valuable than another.

She was murdered leaving me with a daughter to raise. I could not do it alone on my meagre United Nations salary. I was angry and blamed the obvious culprit, China. So, I joined the military, they quickly provided my own department in the neuro-warfare division.'

'I'm sorry.'

'Do not be sorry for me Lieutenant, I will pay for my crimes, pity my daughter for I fear my hatred and lust for revenge have tainted her soul.

She looked up to me and despite my efforts she wanted nothing but to work beside her father. I hoped it was a passing phase but like her mother she is a stubborn woman and when decided on her path not even I could discourage her.'

Sen took another drag on his last smoke and gave Victor a teary-eyed stare, 'I came here knowing she would follow me, I wanted to break the shackles of the past. I fear for my daughter, not just her life but her mind. I fear that too long by my side and Nori may become the same monster as her father.'

'And now you're both dead, or as good as,' stated Diana.

'Once reanimate Nori will have a second chance at life, free from my hate and negativity.'

'That's a big if, they don't just take anyone for reanimation.'

'My daughter is not just anyone Miss Zeng. My daughter is a genius in her field, one day I fully expect her to make a discovery, to push the boundaries of knowledge beyond that of today.'

'I'm sure we'll all be doing handstands the moment she's brought aboard,' replied Diana in a sardonic tone.

'They took you, didn't they?'

'What's that supposed to mean?'

Sen closed his eyelids for a moment, permitting his trained emotional response to drain before reopening them, 'Forgive me.'

'Besides who says she won't get a bullet in the head once she's reanimated?' Sen fixed his eyes upon Diana in an iron stare.

'That's enough Dee,' said Victor.

'Enough? He butchered thousands of innocent people and I'm supposed to get all weepy because of some bullshit story he's spinning to save his daughter?'

'If you forgive others when they sin against you, your heavenly father with forgive you.'

'Oh come on Vic, you don't believe in that shit!'

'But you take it seriously, isn't that what's important?'

'That's different.'

'No it isn't, you're feeling the same hate, the same desire for revenge that led him down his path. Don't let it consume you like it did him, you're better than that Dee,' Victor held the woman he loves by her hand.

Sen took a drag on his smoke before interrupting the lovers, 'Perhaps there is something I can give you Specialist Zeng.'

Diana turned her eyes from the face of the man she loves to one she detests, 'What could you possibly give me?'

'You may execute me, it is the least I can do considering the pain I have caused.'

Diana let go of Victor's hand and unsecured her rifle, 'Now that's the first good idea you've had all day.'

'Allow me to finish my coffee and cigarette.'

Quetz entered the room with a packet of morphine tablets, 'Found.'

'Leave it on the side,' stated Diana as she loaded a round into the chamber of her N-13.

'You're not going to do this?' whispered Victor.

'Damn right I'm gonna do this.'

'You're always talking about spiritual stuff and philosophy.'

'Yeh and you know what Sartre said?'

'No but I'm sure you're gonna tell me and I'm sure I'm not gonna like it.'

'Passiveness serves no other purpose than to put you on the side of the oppressor.'

Victor snorted in disdain.

'What?'

71

'Pretty absurd considering he's a Frenchman!'

'Yeh well, no-one said his countrymen read any of his books, did they?'

'Please Lieutenant,' said Sen as he stubbed out his cigarette, 'She deserves her revenge, besides, now I know how Jesus must have felt.'

Victor's brow furrowed as did his entire forehead, he replied in a sceptical tone, 'Excuse me?'

'When he waited in the garden of Gethsemane.'

'You'll have to run that by me again because I don't recognise the correlation.'

'Knowing he would be arrested and executed he could have fled but instead he had the courage to stare his fate, his death in the face, sacrificing himself for the sins of mankind.'

'Ready when you are,' stated Diana as she aimed down the barrel of her N-13 at Sen's forehead.

'I will offer my life so others can live without sin, executed by my accusers on the cross of hatred and ...'

*BANG*

The rear of Sen's skull blew out painting the wall behind with a melange of colours and textures worthy of any Jackson Pollock.

Victor stood aghast for a second until he spoke in a sublime voice, 'What a jerk.'

# Chapter Eight

Diana dragged Sen's corpse to the cargo hold. Victor moved the Drax and Quetz shifted Huat.

Diana dumped Sen's sticky mess in a far corner, 'Good riddance!'

Victor chucked the Drax on top, 'Twice.'

Quetz discarded his friend's split carcass as yesterday's trash. For a very spiritual people he seemed rather cold.

'Aren't you gonna say anything?' asked Victor.

'Say?' replied Quetz.

'Well he was your friend, isn't there some sort of ceremony or burial rights?'

Quetz grasped Huat's vial, 'Spirit preserve, take to ancestral tomb when Tizapan liberated.'

'That could be a long time.'

Quetz displayed what Victor could only assume was a smile, not that he knew what a lizard's smile resembled, 'Quetz wait, Huat wait.'

'Okay, let's check these sleeper tubes,' he pointed at a tube containing Sen's daughter, 'Check her life signs.'

Diana examine the unit's side, 'Barely registering.'

'Alright I want you and Quetz to hide that tube between the ceiling and hull. Make sure it's completely secure before you weld that hole shut, understood?'

'Sure,' Diana wasn't happy at all.

'I made a promise Dee.'

'I know but ...'

'There are no buts, he brought us the click, gave his life in exchange for his daughter, and I intend to keep my promise come hell or high water.'

Diana nodded her head, she wasn't going to argue any further for it would do no good. Victor was a man of virtue, a man of conviction and most of all a man of conscience. Conviction the ocean in which he swam, conscience the

73

oxygen he breathed, he'd truly die if deprived of either. Victor could no more go back on his word than a whale not surface for air.

Diana checked each tube, while she did so Quetz spoke in Victor's ear.
'Quetz see grey ghost defeat black beast, grey ghost brave, bravest of all creatures.'
'Gee thanks,' replied Victor in a sardonic tone.
'Quetz say one day either be no Drax or no human. Quetz hope no Drax.'
'Hope?'
'Hope.'
'The desire that something might happen without you actually doing anything to make it so?'
'Quetz do what Quetz can.'
'Yeh, but you cretins ... canarks, are gonna have to man up if you want those bastards off your planet. The only way to win freedom is to take it yourself, with a gun in one hand and your enemies beating heart in the other. If someone swoops in to do it for you, you're swapping one master for another, do you understand?'
'Quetz understand, Quetz not know how.'
'Buy some weapons, stockpile them, supply your resistance, that'd be a start.'
'Who sell weapons?'
'That's your problem my friend.'
'Okay the tubes are secure,' stated Diana.
'Good, get Nori tucked away.'
'You're on a first name basis now?'
'Dee!'
'Uuurrrhhh!'
Victor lit a cigarette while they moved her tube inside Coatl's under skin. As the freighter drifted toward Shinko's lab he glared ominously on a Drax sleeper tube.

To stretch the now thin oxygen supply Dee would inhabit Sen's tube and he'd take the remaining Drax tube. With his reanimated physiology Victor might tolerate its atmosphere. Nanobots in his blood would purge toxins from his blood stream. They worked when boarding a Drax vessel, however, they'd never been tested in a sleeper tube.

As far as Victor understood there was no reason to fear. In fact, its atmosphere should have a less toxic affect since Victor's life signs would be reduced to a minimum, he'd require but a tiny amount of oxygen while nanites worked at full strength.

After securing Nori's tube the three sat down for a last supper, so to speak. Coffee and cigarettes for Vic, lattes for Dee and Quetz.

'Can you believe that asshole, comparing himself to Jesus in the garden of Gethsemane?' said Diana.

'The scary thing is I think he believed it,' replied Victor.

'What Gethsemane?'

'It's the place Jesus was arrested.'

'Who Jesus?'

'A religious figure, for Christians.'

'Humans are Christians?'

'Not all humans, there are many religions on Earth.'

'Why?'

Victor displayed a blank expression, he'd never considered the question before now, 'I guess that's just the way it is. If you can't get everyone to agree on their favourite coffee how the hell are they gonna agree on the same God?'

'Foolish, Tizapan one belief.'

Victor took a long drag on his cigarette, inhaling deeply before blowing out smoke as Vesuvius on a rough day, 'Pity, a few nasty religious wars, you might've been mean enough to resist the Drax.'

Diana rolled her eyes while Quetz moved his head from side to side in that quizzical fashion ingrained into all his species, 'Not understand.'

'Never mind, it was a bad joke.'

'Human like to fight, why?'

Victor took a sip of coffee, relaxing into his chair, 'We don't like to fight, conflict is in our nature. It's like giving birth or visiting the mother in law at thanksgiving, you do it because it's necessary.'

'Curious, human fight because necessary.'

'That's why the Drax want us dead, anyone in their space that strives for liberty and justice gets bombed into the stone age then eradicated. You canarks aren't aggressive by nature, you don't thrive on conflict you thrive on peace and unity, that's why you still exist, but only as slaves.'

'You defeat Drax, we become human slaves?'

'If you don't learn to fight for your freedom, maybe.'


Nori had been hidden from prying eyes, Coatl's remaining crew gathered in the cargo hold. Victor and Diana stripped to their underwear. Weapons disarmed and passed to Quetz they prepared to enter sleepers.

Victor observed fear in his fiancé's eyes, taking her hands Victor reassured Diana, 'Don't worry Dee, we'll make it.'

'Sure.'

Victor leant down and pressed his lips against hers, she let go of his hands wrapping her arms around him. Diana maintained a grip, afraid this moment may be the last.

A combination of affection and agony passed from her lips to his as a secret note at a masquerade ball. For a moment he felt guilty, guilty he'd caused such heart wrenching pain in the woman he loved.

But Victor overcame that feeling for should he break his word he'd be wracked with the same guilt for the rest of his existence and he knew Diana would think less of him despite inevitable denials.

They parted lips, he spoke softly to a woman on the verge of tears, 'It'll be fine.'

'And if it isn't?'

'Maybe you'll get a promotion,' jested Victor.

'Vic, you're not funny.'

'Sorry, I just don't know what to say.'

'Get inside the tube, I'll make sure your life signs are steady.'

He nodded his head and peered at Quetz, 'Thanks.'

'For what?' answered the four-armed alien.

'Doctor Sen wasn't the only good judge of character.'

'Thank you, grey ghost, for trusting Quetz.'

Victor kissed Diana again, he felt energy transfer between them. One might have concluded love did pulse at a certain wavelength and their hearts had found it, hitting its beat as one, playing a duet.

They parted and Victor entered his stasis tube, the capsule door swung around to encase him. Its thick, predominantly Drax atmosphere, difficult to breath. His last recollection was staring into Diana's eyes through misty glass. She no more than a worried little girl wrangling her hands, snatching quick glances at the read out.


'Vic? Can you hear me? Vic, can you hear me?'

Victor's eyes opened, his lids heavy, a pair of portcullises hauled up in winter. Finally they opened to a blear of light. He tried to raise his hand for shade but it didn't move. Again he pushed and slowly it rose as a medieval drawbridge.

'Vic, can you hear me?'

Victor tried to speak but his throat contracted, a wispy sound exited its dry cave, 'Yes.'

'Quetz, help me.'

Victor felt himself man handled, carried as a hurt child, for how far he didn't know, until he lay down head propped by pillows.

'Drink this.'

Victor sensed the edge of a cup press his bottom lip, a warm brew of coffee filled both nostrils, exciting taste buds before exploding on the back of his throat. Victor's windpipe expanded soaking up liquid as a dry sponge dropped into a bath.

'Uuuhhh!' spluttered Zellmann.

'Drink it!' shouted a voice Victor recognised to be Diana.

Victor's vision cleared presenting the most beautiful sight, not an angel but as good as. So concerned with his health she hadn't bothered to dress before resurrecting Victor from his Drax coffin. Her face shone as salvation to shipwrecked sailors. A beauty rarely witnessed, a rapture not experienced in a man's heart until that moment of delivery. Sights such as Diana do cause men who once scorned the existence of God to convert to devout believers, that was Diana's splendid visage.

She slapped his cheek, 'Can you see me?'

He sat up, 'Yeh.'

Diana's smiling eyes watered in joy.

'What happened?'

'We'll dock in five minutes.'

'How are you?'

'Okay now,' smiled the Specialist.

'Maybe we should get some clothes on?'

'You're such a party pooper,' quipped Diana.

He looked down at her tight cotton bra, 'I was right, it is chilly in those tubes.'

She kissed her beau, he felt the pulse of relief blended with love, an exquisite rice wine so potent it would open any man's eyes … and heart. Diana's release alerted Victor's body, everything had gone as projected, and so he passed the same spirit to the lip of her cup.

After parting Victor looked up at Quetz, an expression of disgust filled his face.

'Something wrong?'

'Feel sick.'

'Why's that?'

'Touch female, revolting, depraved.'

He smiled, 'So why'd you keep watching?'

Diana chuckled as Quetz exited the sleeping quarters in a huff.

The marines dressed and checked weapons. Quetz had piloted the Coatl on an ever-thinning atmosphere before making contact using his ship's landing lights.

The Coatl was towed into a landing bay.

Victor watched as they entered the jaws of a city in space. This instillation resembled two blocks of New York city clumped together. Antennae pushed from above and below, depending on your orientation, for these celestial sky scrapers punched out from both ends of its blocky centre.

Lights faded, shadows consumed the Coatl as a mauve flower obscuring the morning sun. Victor put a reassuring hand on Quetz's shoulder, 'Good job.'

'They're gonna be pissed,' stated Diana.

'I guess that's just tough.'

'What're you gonna tell them?'

'I think President Kennedy said it best: life isn't fair.'


The Coatl's airlock opened, men standing by took one whiff of its foul atmosphere and turned away in disgust. A rescue team attached breather masks yet before engaging a tall dark figure appeared from an alien gloom.

Teams of armed men drew weapons and braced, 'HALT!'

Victor raised his hands.

'Place your weapon on the ground and move away.'

Victor complied.

Combat ready guards hurried in, 'is anyone else on the ship?'

'Specialist Zeng and a canark.'

'Is the craft secure?'

Victor observed the man's uniform, carbon nano weave plates protected his shins, thighs, groin, torso and arms, 'Everything's secure, Sergeant.'

The guard lowered his rifle and saluted, 'Sorry sir.'

Victor returned his salute, 'At ease, your cargo escaped and was destroyed in the ensuing fire fight Sergeant.'

'Understood sir.'

Victor stepped past the Sergeant and out of the airlock followed by Diana and Quetz.

Victor sat in a small ornate office decorated in the Japanese style. A suit of Samurai armour on a mannequin captured light, polished with meticulous care. A set of medieval swords flashed photons across the room, their blades as clean as a Buckingham Palace toilet seat. Victor was of no doubt these weapons were the real McCoy. On the desk before him rested a copy of the Bushido Shoshinshu (the code of the samurai) alongside Shakespeare's Hamlet.

A door opened and closed, Victor stood to witness Laertes Shinko, 'You may sit Lieutenant.'

Victor relaxed into his chair, Laertes remained standing, 'I have read your report Lieutenant. My father will be disappointed.'

'I'm sorry, I had no choice.'

'I understand, what puzzles me is the location of the third sleeper tube.'

'Third tube?'

'Yes, it was loaded into the Coatl yet failed to materialize on arrival.'

'Must've been a mistake.'

'I assure you there was no mistake Lieutenant Zellmann.'

'Ah you know how it is with these flexi pushing ...'

'No, I don't Lieutenant Zellmann. A third tube was aboard because I supervised its loading. I sealed the hold personally. Do you have any explanation as to how or where it vanished to?'

'I guess it'll have to remain a mystery.'

Laertes' voice and stare co-ordinated to fashion repressed anger, a common trait in the Shinko family, 'Do not trifle with me Lieutenant.'

Victor took out a packet of cigarettes, 'I'm a cheesecake man myself.'

'Your humour is not appreciated Lieutenant. I am responsible for that cargo, when my father discovers it has been spoiled, I shall be punished.'

'Spoiled? You mean went berserk and tried to kill everyone aboard.'

'If that pilot had not been so incompetent ...'

80

'Well that's not my fault is it? I was there for security and when your illegal cargo went nuts and killed the other half and the co-pilot my options became severely limited.'

'On that point, Doctor … the occupant of the human sleeper tube,' Laertes slapped a flexi in front of Victor, 'died of a single fatal gunshot wound to the head.'

'There was a fire fight we had to take it down.'

'My medical staff believe it to have been fired from an N-13, at point blank range, can you explain that Lieutenant Zellmann?'

Victor lit his cigarette and snorted out its first fresh plume, an American peacock beshadowing the Japanese pheasant, 'What can I say? Life's a bitch!'

'WHO FIRED THAT BULLET LIEUTENANT?'

Victor smirked, 'Huat.'

'WHO?'

'The co-pilot fired the shot. I was knocked off my feet by the Drax, my weapon left my grip, Huat picked it up and fired hitting the occupant of the second tube in the head. The Drax turned on him and Specialist Zeng put the animal down while it savaged the co-pilot, it's all in my report.'

Laertes narrowed his eyes on Victor and hissed in a defiant tone, 'I don't believe you Lieutenant.'

Victor stood up and stared down Laertes, he the matador filled with confidence, Laertes the bull replete with aggression, 'Both the pilot and Specialist Zeng will corroborated my report.'

'You are all liars.'

'Does that include you and your father?'

Laertes eyes widened in uncontrolled anger, 'HOW DARE YOU!'

'I'm not the one smuggling contraband aliens and giving safe harbour to a mass murderer on Asia's most wanted list.'

Laertes cooled into a satisfied grin, 'So you did kill him.'

'Let's just say justice caught up and leave it at that.'

'Shinko Refineries will not bring Necron Industries to a legal tribunal, however, I will not forget this Lieutenant.'

81

'Is that it?'
'For now Lieutenant.'

# Chapter Nine

The Coatl returned to Cloud 9 for repairs. Victor spent his time working out how he might smuggle Nori aboard Necron. Afterwards came the task of transferring her to Medical. He'd decided to tackle each excursion one at a time.

Once docked he and Diana disembarked, a customs guard blocked their path, 'Weapons not permitted,' hissed a canark.

Victor held out his hand awaiting the agent's identity pad. The canark pressed its pad against his hand. Victor's identity and clearance to carry firearms aboard Cloud 9 was certified.

The customs agent didn't like it yet he moved aside, 'You pass.'

Victor moved forward but the agent blocked Diana, 'Not female!'

Diana bared her hand, customs executed the same process, 'You pass.'

Diana smiled, 'There's a good little boy.'

Victor guessed that was a reptilian sneer but he couldn't be certain, still, who cared? They'd made it back in one piece despite a meteorite, a crazy scientist and psychopathic alien. It was good to be alive or as alive as a Necron Marine could be.

While strolling the outer promenade a commotion kicked up. Victor's attention was drawn to a large rabble consisting of canarks brandishing knives, pieces of broken pipe and night sticks aimed at a fleeing human clutching a small bag for dear life.

The stumbling man made eye contact with Victor, the Lieutenant recognised his Tech Specialist. Nass charged for Lieutenant Zellmann, Billy's desperate visage transmitted a story of woe.

On reaching the Lieutenant Nass saluted and between gasps implored, 'Sir ... help!'

The crowd caught up, Victor stood between both parties, N-13 directed groundward, for now, 'There a problem gentlemen?'

A canark dressed in a flashy green and white jacket, satin trousers and shirt with overblown cravat hissed, 'Give thief.'

'I'm sorry?'

'Human steal from casino, use nano-bots, nano-bots prohibited, cheat Verik out of tax credit.'

Several four-armed reptiles flanked them, prepared to give Specialist Nass a beating.

'Is this true Specialist?'

'I, I ...'

'Hand your winnings back Specialist.'

'But they're mine.'

Victor turned to Nass, 'And now they're mine and I'm telling you to hand them over to this guy, is that understood Specialist?'

Billy begrudgingly transferred his winnings, 'Yes sir.'

Victor fixed his gaze on the four-armed proprietor and a band of staff armed to the teeth with melee weapons, 'Okay?'

The owner checked its contents, 'Tax credits returned, now retribution.'

'Retribution?'

'Customer steal from Verik, Verik beat customer.'

Diana chuckled, 'Beat your mother, beat your customers, it's no wonder they call you guys cretins!'

'SILENCE FEMALE!'

Diana positioned her N-13 barrel on his crotch area, 'Or what, numb nuts?'

Victor spoke calmly to Verik, 'You've got your money, and his, so why don't you go back to your shit hole before she blows your balls off?'

Verik sneered, 'Grey ghost arrogant, grey ghost meet Drax not so arrogant.'

Victor kicked the owner as hard as he could in the groin. Verik fell to the ground, casino chips splurged across the promenade.

Chips splashed as a wave upon a Californian beach and a scream went out, "SURF'S UP!". Otherwise sane creatures became hysterical in a mad scramble for free cash.

Casino staff eyed one another nervously. Verik writhed on the floor, clenching his genitals in a foetal position, mumbling to ancestors. Staff dashed ... not for Victor ... but for as many chips as they might stuff their pockets with. Being a canark, four hands and four pockets offered a serious edge over humans.

Billy went for his share yet Victor grabbed his shirt collar snapping him back as a rubber band, 'Nass, you're coming with me.'

'But sir, the chips!'

'Nass.'

'Yes sir?'

'Shut the fuck up!'

'Yes sir.'

The three departed a scene of utter pandemonium. Cloud 9's public were going wild. For that moment usually stable, decent people, lost all control, lurching for free money dispersed along an area of about six metres squared. Station staff, rather than break it up joined in a disgusting orgy of greed.

Specialist Nass turned back to observe, his winnings spread as a whore's legs while a frenzied mob fought for her love.

'That's a bad habit you got there Nass.'

'Yes sir.'

'It'd be a pity if I mentioned this incident in my report to Captain Gibson.'

Nass went a little white, 'Sir?'

'Lucky for you I need your help.'

Billy yielded a sigh of relief, 'Sir?'

Victor stopped walking to scrutinize his ward, 'Do we have a deal Specialist?'

'What do you need sir?'

'I need to get a sleeper tube aboard Necron ... undetected.'

Billy shook his head, 'No way!'

'Fine,' Victor carried on walking.

'Sir, stop!'

Victor halted.

'I could put it on the manifest for the next cargo delivery.'

85

'When's that?'

'I don't know but they've been shipping replacement parts aboard since you left. I reckon you could sneak it in that way … but …'

'But what?'

'I'd need access to the mainframe and I don't have that, sir.'

'Could you hack in?'

Nass pulled an uncomfortable visage, his eyes shifted left and right.

'Come on Nass, can you do it?'

'I reckon I could but if I get caught, I'll be harvested.'

'You hack in and get that tube on the manifest then send me the details. If they come looking for you I'll cover your ass, understood?'

'But Cloud 9, they have a separate manifest and …'

'I'll sort it this end.'

'If you don't mind sir, what's in it for me?'

'I don't report your criminal acts aboard Cloud 9.'

'Criminal?'

'Premeditated fraud, you do know the punishment for that here?'

'No?'

'Convicted criminals are spaced … choose your poison Mr Nass.'

Billy shrugged his shoulders and spat in a defeated tone, 'Fuck my life!'

Large crates coloured by content were shifted onto loaders. Imagine a six wheeled forklift truck yet it employed a clamp, permitting the vehicle to hold cargo in place even in zero gravity.

Men in grey boiler suits rushed to and fro in what one might believe chaos yet chaos did not reign here for these fellows understood their business fluently. A foreman barked orders as workers took directions shifting Necron's supplies onto a Blackbird.

'Pete! Get the fucking distributors this time will ya?' shouted a fat guy chewing a cigar while ticking items off his flexi.

'Sure,' replied the forklift operator.

'And Pete!'

'WHAT?'

A hullabaloo of machinery groaned under the weight of supply crates as the noise of motors whining pushed from one place to another.

'Do it speedy like, last thing I need is one of them creepy zombies ridding my butt!'

'Excuse me?'

The foreman turned 180 degrees to witness a tall figure emerge from shadowy red light spilling into the bay. On closer examination he realised its true nature, a zombie.

'Hey fella, no offence intended it was just an expression, you know?'

'None taken.'

'You want something?'

'I'm here to supervise the transfer of a supply item, seven B.'

'Seven B ya say?' The foreman examined his flexi, 'sorry bub, no seven B here.'

Victor stood to one side, 'You must've missed it.'

The foreman looked past Victor to witness a sleeper tube obscured by crimson light, 'Listen bub if it ain't on my flexi it don't go on the ship, got it?'

'I'm here to put it on your flexi, bub.'

'I wasn't told about this before.'

'Well you're being told now.'

The foreman approached the tube, he peered within, a woman's face contorted in horror while a pale complexion and puncture wounds rounded off her gruesome tale.

He removed his cigar and coughed, 'Forget it bub.'

Victor handed the foreman a flexi, 'Do your job and put it on that bird.'

'She been through quarantine?'

'Sure.'

'Where's the documentation?'

'Okay, how much?'

'How much what?'

'To get this tube on board.'

One of the workers overheard, stopped what he was doing and locked his gaze upon the pair.

The foreman sneered, 'I'm an honest man, I don't take money from no-one,' he turned to the worker, 'get back to work asshole!'

The bay worker moved on, after he'd cleared earshot the foreman spoke in a hushed tone, 'Keep ya voice down will ya?'

Victor grinned, 'So, how much?'

'What tax rights ya carrying?'

'Indian?'

'I don't take that funny money.'

'United States?'

The foreman raised an eyebrow while chugging his cigar.

'Fine, Japanese.'

The foreman's lips formed a smile around his cigar before he removed it from his mouth, 'Now we're talking … five hundred?'

'Sure,' Victor picked a small golden disc from his pocket, tapped it on his inner wrist and offered it to the foreman.

'Fuck! I shoulda asked for a thousand!' said the fellow accepting his bribe. The foreman turned back to his driver, 'HEY PETE!'

'What the fuck now?'

'Get this fucking tube on the bird will ya?'

'Gimme a break Al, I'm backed up already!'

'If this tube's on the next flight I'm buying beers tonight.'

Pete's truck flew across the bay toward the tube, 'This the one?'

'Yup.'

'What the fuck happened to her?'

'Drax got her,' stated Victor.

'Pity, she's got nice tits.'

Both Al and Pete chuckled.

Victor folded his arms, 'You fellas want to watch your backs.'

'What's the fuck's that supposed to mean?' said the foreman.

'Well you know Drax read their surroundings via sound?'

'Sure everyone knows that.'

'Well it seems certain sounds carry better than others and It just so happens their frequencies send Drax into a violent psychopathic frenzy.'

'What fucking sounds?'

'No-one's really sure but certain people are susceptible to attacks. In my experience the guys in my platoon who swore a blue streak bought the farm first. They say this girl here was cursing like a sailor when it jumped out of nowhere and ripped her apart. They didn't even know there was a Drax onboard until it went nuts and sucked her dry.'

Pete and Al exchanged an ominous stare. The foreman fixed his eyes on Victor, 'You serious?'

'As serious as cancer … bub.'


'I was aware of no delivery to Medical today,' mumble Doctor Mendelson scanning his flexi.

'You know how it is.'

'No I do not Lieutenant,' he moved over to the sleeper tube, 'Is she one of yours?'

'I don't understand.'

'Do not insult my intelligence Lieutenant. The last time you were here with a body you held a pistol to my head.'

Victor pulled out a packet of cigarettes only to be blocked by an expression of disapproval. He returned them to his shirt pocket, 'Sorry.'

'The corpse, what am I expected to do with it?'

'You ever heard of Doctor Sen Joshuyo?'

'Of course, the man is a genius. I studied his work on brain-pattern warfare in Russia … it was most helpful,' Mendelson carried his signature creepy expression.

'Then I'd like to introduce you to Nori Joshuyo, his daughter.'

Mendelson lowered a flexi so he might bring his face closer to the sleeper tube's glass, 'Are you sure?'

'Certain.'

'You have piqued my curiosity Lieutenant, however, she has not been registered on Necron's medical database, what do you expect me to do with her?'

'Spare me doc, you're the shiftiest bastard on this ship. I'd bet you're running half a dozen illegal operations right under the Brass' nose.'

Mendelson turned from Nori's twisted expression to Zellmann, 'Be careful with your words Lieutenant.'

Victor handed Mendelson a flexi, 'This is the last will and testament of Doctor Sen Joshuyo.'

Mendelson took the document, 'He is dead?'

'As a door nail but his daughter might be reanimated.'

'For what purpose Lieutenant?'

'She has a PhD in …'

Mendelson scoffed, 'Pah, every man and woman on my deck has a PhD Lieutenant! Perhaps she should apply for the Marine Corps?'

'She was Sen's assistant, she worked on his mind control program. Sen was on his way to Shinko's lab with Nori and a Drax, a Drax he had under full mental control,' Mendelson's attention shifted to Zellmann, 'He and the Drax died in an accident, in short he sacrificed his life so his daughter might live. In exchange for her life you get his research and his daughter, who according to him is the only one able to translate it properly.'

Mendelson scanned the document, 'Hmm, and what would prevent me from taking this research and harvesting his dear daughter?'

'Me,' stated Victor in an ominous tone.

Mendelson smirked, 'Is that a threat Lieutenant?'

'You might have that device on your wrist Doc but there's a few men in my platoon aware of our little conversation and if I were to mysteriously die …'

'You mean your girlfriend, Specialist Zeng.'

'Perhaps, but there's only one way to find out, or you could just reanimate Nori.'

'As you know it is not my decision Lieutenant.'

'I don't think anyone's gonna notice an extra scientist, that's assuming you haven't pulled this stunt in the past.'

Mendelson moved to a medical station and began to tap it, 'Let me see, Nori Jushuyo, apparently she was a lead scientist under Sen Jushuyo in Japan's neuro-warfare department. She received several honours for her part in the Shanghai massacre of 2684, hmmm, perhaps she has some potential?'

The Shanghai massacre of 2684 was a brutal employment of brainwave warfare in the closing year of the Sino war. Japan's allies had deserted her while China pushed them off the continent. As Chinese forces prepared for a final bloody assault it became obvious Shanghai was indefensible.

The military began to pull out, a scramble to reach ships and carriers before the horde struck. Sen saw it as an opportunity to test his technology.

Once Japanese forces had made it to safety, transmissions began. Transmitting brainwaves from several sources throughout the city, Chinese citizens turned on one another. Anarchy ensued, men and women who'd never met tore at one another in the street as wild animals.

The Chinese army had each and every one of its soldiers chipped with counter measures to the device yet it was not always so. Early on the weapon was very effective against China's armed forces. However, Japan's allies threatened to withdraw unless its use was discontinued. The government, much to Sen's ire, restricted its use since the U.N had deemed it inhumane.

By 2684 The U.S.A and her stooges had suffered enough, they no longer supported Japan with frontline troops, permitting China time to formulate a method of protection.

These facts did not discourage Doctor Sen for they couldn't chip every single man, woman and child in China. His neuro-warfare created havoc amongst highly populated areas along China's coast, and now that Shanghai was to fall he set the dogs loose on one another, buying his people time to slip away as thieves in the night.

China would not attack while civilians murdered one another in the streets, they'd tried before and learnt their lesson. Forcing soldiers to kill countrymen just to get at a few Japs shattered morale more so than losing a battle.

Sen and his daughter received the order of the rising sun in honour of their achievements, preventing a massacre of Japanese soldiers by creating one amongst Chinese civilians.

Sen was respected in his homeland yet despised outside her borders. Honoured by the Emperor and every military General alive he was a scientific superstar. When the war was over his presence became a stain Japan's government couldn't remove.

For Japan to move on Sen's sacrifice was required. Members of his government arranged his escape to the only place he could hide, space.

Nori refused to leave her father, persisting by his side, ending up at Shinko Refineries.

Guilt ripped Sen like a beast tearing at its master's heart, not due to the butchery he was complicit in but his daughter. He'd destroyed her future, how could she find love, settle down and create a family now?

He was complicit in the assassination of Nori's life, he'd discarded her chance at happiness, thrown her life into the gutter to pursue his own personal lust for revenge.

Only when faced with death on the Coatl was Sen forced to confront reality. For years he'd hidden it but when the light of truth shone in his eyes Sen embraced it. The only way his daughter could be happy and have a life was to sacrifice his own.

# Chapter Ten

On entering Medical Victor's heart jumped a little, Colonel Rockey received a check-up, supervised by Nori.

Diana was puzzled at the sight, she knew Victor had smuggled her aboard but was unaware of if or when she'd be reanimated.

Rockey complained in an irritated southern accent, 'Where's Mendelson?'

'He is busy Colonel,' replied Nori.

'I get my yearly check-up from Mendelson, I don't trust you damn foreigners!'

The Colonel rolled up his sleeve before a nurse took a blood sample whilst medical units monitored nanites.

'But Colonel, Doctor Mendelson is Russian.'

'You know what I mean! I don't trust you slanty eyed bastards, never did, just as likely to stick a knife in my back than take my blood pressure.'

'Yes, you have very high blood pressure … and I'm taking into account that you're a corpse,' Nori smiled but to no affect.

'You try commanding twelve hundred men that haven't had pussy in six months!'

Nori raised her eyebrows, 'Really Colonel there's no need to be so gauche.'

'Gauche? I don't speak Chinese!'

Nori tapped her medical pad, noting his biological readouts, 'Tell me Colonel are you this antagonistic as a rule or are you going out of your way for me?'

'What are you a psyche?'

'If I were you'd have been sectioned by now.'

Colonel Rockey couldn't believe she'd spoken to him in such a condescending manner … that was his shtick, 'Where the hell's Mendelson?'

'You've asked that question seven times already and received the same answer each time Colonel, now shut up and hold your arm still so the nurse may receive a reliable sample.'

'My arm's as steady as rock!'

'It suits you Colonel.'

'What the hell's that supposed to mean?'

'You remind of a rock Colonel, obstinate and utterly dense.'

'Ahem.'

Nori and Rockey turned to see Victor and Diana.

'Never thought I'd be glad to see you Zellmann. Find Mendelson and get him here now, before this chink has me harvested!'

'You may disregard that order Lieutenant,' came a Russian accent from an adjoining office.

Mendelson stepped into the examination room.

'You been here all the time?' bellowed Rockey.

'I'm putting Doctor Joshuyo through her paces Colonel and who better to do that for me?'

'Well her bedside manner stinks!'

'Yours leaves much to be desired Colonel.'

'Damn doctors, you people have got nothing better to do than stick your needles in me and tell me to eat shitty food.'

Nori looked up from her pad, 'It could be worse Colonel, I might recommend you for a rectal examination.'

Victor laughed under his breath until Rockey's iron stare met with his joyous visage, killing it instantly.

'I wouldn't let some chink humiliate ME by poking around my ass!'

'Trust me Colonel the larger part of any humiliation would be mine!'

Rockey sneered at Nori then addressed Mendelson, 'What's with her? She got a PhD in shit talking?'

'I do apologise Colonel but as I said Doctor Joshuyo is new here.'

'I don't remember any new medical staff coming aboard, not in years.'

Mendelson's eyes flicked to Victor then backed to Rockey. The Colonel noticed Mendelson's momentary lapse, something wasn't quite right.

'Doctor Joshuyo has been in stasis for some time Colonel.'

'Why's that?' asked Rockey in a cautious tone.

'A few days ago one of my staff died in a tragic accident. Doctor Joshuyo was revived in order to fill his opening.'

'How'd he die?'

'It seems he overdosed on crash.'

'Crash? What the hell was he doing with that shit?'

'Toxicology says he was a long-term addict. A large amount of the drug was found in his quarters.'

'And you never picked it up?'

'Unfortunately not, I was just as shocked as the rest of my staff. I believe he employed a masking agent to hide the substance from me.'

'Any reason you picked a chink?'

'Doctor Joshuyo was formerly employed by the Japanese government in their NJ-OUTRE programme, during the Sino-war.'

Rockey leapt from his seat, 'WHAT!?' pulled the needle out his arm and rolled down his sleeve, 'ARE YOU CRAZY?'

'I'm sorry Colonel?'

'SHE'S A BRAIN BUTCHER!'

'I'm not aware of that term Colonel.'

Nori intervened, 'He is correct Doctor Mendelson. Our allies, the allies that deserted us, used that term to describe those involved in the neuro-warfare arm of the military. They prevented us from employing brainwave emitters against enemy troops. We would have been victorious had our government ignored the weak Americans … excuse me Colonel, I meant no offence.'

Rockey stepped away, 'She doesn't come near me again, you got that Mendelson?'

'Colonel that war is over, Doctor Joshuyo is an employee of Necron Industries now.'

'I don't care if she's the Virgin Mother Mary, keep her away from me, you understand?'

'I understand Colonel.'

Rockey grabbed his tunic, storming out the examination room. As he left medical staff gawped. The entire deck equally shocked by the revelation.

Nori was unfazed by Colonel Rockey, she'd experienced this reaction many times over. She turned to Victor, 'Lieutenant?'

'Lieutenant Zellmann.'

'THE Lieutenant Zellmann?'

Victor made an uncomfortable grin, 'Is there another?'

She looked at her superior, Mendelson nodded his head.

'Please sit Lieutenant.'

Victor took Rockey's seat as a nurse scanned him.

'Please roll your sleeve up Lieutenant.'

The nurse inserted a needle and began to draw blood.

'It seems I am in your debt Lieutenant.'

'How so?'

'My father left a record, a last will and testament, he credited you with saving my life.'

'What record?'

She pointed to her head, 'A chip in my brain, he has … had one also. The record was sent and information stored for examination on revival,' she glanced at Diana, 'You are Specialist Zeng.'

'Aren't you a clever girl,' snapped Diana.

'My father was an angry man, he blamed the Chinese for his woes in life. I hold no such animosity toward you or your kind Miss Zeng.'

'Well I don't know about you Vic but that's me reassured,' replied Diana in a sardonic tone.

Nori grinned as she examined her medical pad, 'So many cynical people in one place, my father would be pleased.'

'Why's that?' asked Victor.

'Scepticism is the foundation of good science, if it were otherwise new and better theories could not arise, expanding the bounds of knowledge, unlocking the full potential of humanity.'

Diana folded her arms, intent on a confrontation with Nori, 'Does that include me?'

96

'Unlike my father I do not hold the belief that Chinese are a subset of the human race. Nor do I believe they are genetically inferior, unable to break their biological chains and rise to the same status as I.'

Diana maintained a suspicious tone, 'I guess the massacre of Shanghai gave you a revelation?'

'No, it is quite simple, they defeated us. If they are to be sub-humans unable to err on the side of logic and reason, the logical conclusion is we must be inferior. An uncomfortable fact my people were unwilling to face, a possibility they refused to entertain before or after the war.'

Diana was stunned to be in the presence of a Japanese who not only faced the facts but aired them publicly.

'I see from your expression you are surprised Specialist. Don't be, I am a scientist not a fantasist. I am meticulous in my examination of evidence my only interest is truth, no matter how uncomfortable.'

'So what's your conclusion about the Sino-war?'

Nori nodded at her nurse who began removing Victor's needle, 'The premise for the war was faulty. Nevertheless it had no bearing on ultimate victory. We failed to attain victory, not because we didn't possess the means, but because we didn't possess the will. My government was filled with weak fools who bent to the will of foreigners … as a cheap whore for sailors!'

Victor cleared his throat, reminding the young lady she was in the company of gentlemen. If she heard him she didn't betray it, for Nori was as forthright as her father.

Sen despised the Chinese because they'd killed his wife. Nori despised her own people because they'd launched an attempt to conquer the Chinese coast and subdue its government yet refused to do what was necessary to attain that goal. Her hatred for their weakness burnt inside.

She and her father had provided the required tools but the Americans threatened to withdraw support after witnessing its effects for the first time. Just as McArthur had requested the use of nuclear weapons in Korea. A nuclear bombing campaign that would push into China, defeating them once and for all. The American government blocked its own path to victory.

97

Again, the Japanese military pressed for the use of Sen's neuron transmitter, only to have their route blocked.

By the time America had withdrawn and the government approved its use China's military had countered Sen's weapon.

Every Chinese soldier had been chipped, blocking external brainwave patterns, and so it became a terror weapon used on civilians.

Nori set the past in the past, for a new life had begun, a life aboard the Necron where she would fight a new enemy no longer held back by stuffy old men afraid of public opinion. For Doctor Mendelson made it clear, against Drax, anything goes. They weren't human, they were evil beasts from the depths of hell. No experiment was too twisted when it came to this vile species, no weapon too shocking, too destructive, too indiscriminate.

Nori had found her true place in the universe. Not only had Doctor Mendelson given the green light for Nori's thought control experiments but he participated. Perhaps it would lead to what Doctor Sen had dreamt of, however, its victim would not be Chinese, its victim would be Drax.

'I see the crew of this ship and I recognise men of progress willing to push science to its boundaries. That includes you Specialist, and as long as we we are aligned in the same cause I am here to serve you.'

'So, what's the prognosis Doc?' asked Victor.

'Not good Lieutenant. There are far too many toxins in your body.'

'Toxins?'

'You eat too much red meat, alcohol intake is above a marine's recommended three units a week. An addiction to tobacco prevents your nanites from working at full capacity since they're permanently repairing damage. Finally, you indulge far too often in fried foods, you need to cut down, perhaps I can recommend salads instead?'

'SALAD?' shouted Victor in an incredulous tone.

'Your blood stream is teaming with oxidants and free radicals Lieutenant. They reduce nanite efficiency by fifteen percent.'

Victor stood up and rolled his sleeve down, 'I'll try to cut back on french fries.'

Diana began to chuckle. Nori fixed her gaze on Dee, 'If we are to win this war I will require every marine to be operating at full efficiency.'

Victor spoke in a soft voice, 'Sorry to burst your bubble Doc but we aren't in a war. We do jobs for folks, folks with money. As for your advice, I'll give it some thought.'

After a check-up and lecture, Vic and Dee slipped away to catch a few hours with each other. Victor pulled out his cigarettes, Diana's hand blocked the packet, 'I'd rather you didn't.'

'You siding with the doctor?'

'I'd rather kiss a man that didn't taste of stale tobacco.'

He leant down and they kissed, merging inside one another for a moment. They parted lips and he smiled, 'Can I smoke now?'

'I suppose so,' said Dee in a grumpy voice.

Victor lit a cigarette with his green yeonum lighter and took a deep breath, 'It's good to be back.'

'What do you think of Nori?'

Victor hadn't really considered Necron's new addition. He rested against a bulkhead then peered from a tiny porthole, one of few available, 'I guess you can't have too many scientists and doctors, right?'

Diana stood on the other side of the port hole opening onto Cloud 9, her eyebrows raised in a cynical fashion.

'What?'

'Anything else?'

'I don't know, she's a diet Nazi?'

'You were pretty taken with her on the Coatl.'

Victor grinned, now he knew what she was getting at.

'Something funny?'

Victor took another puff on his cigarette then rubbed his chin while peering stoically into space, 'Yeh there's something, but you know I can't quite put my finger on it,' he turned to Diana, 'for some reason I'm feeling chilly.'

'That's the feeling of an empty bed.'

Victor chuckled, 'Come on you're not serious?'

'I don't like her.'

'Why?'

'Because she likes you, she's got her eye on you Vic, I know it.'

'Eye on me? For what?'

'She wants you, a woman can tell.'

'That's crazy.'

Diana looked out the porthole frustrated by Victor's dismissive attitude, 'She'll try to take you from me, I know it.'

He took another drag on his smoke and replied, 'Do you think she's gonna use mind control and force me to grope her?'

Diana narrowed her eyes and snapped in disparaging tone, 'I doubt she'd need to go to those lengths.'

Victor felt rather insulted, 'Are you saying I'm easy?'

'As easy as any man when his genitals override his brain.'

'Gimme a break!'

'It's not your fault, men are all made with the same flaw. I guess it was useful when infant mortality was over fifty percent.'

'Gee thanks, now I don't feel like you've called me an asshole!

'It's just your nature.'

'Man is fully responsible for his nature and his choices.'

Diana turned to Victor, a smile chased away sadness, 'You read Sartre?'

'Only because you kept bugging me. Besides I'm not in the habit of blaming my shitty decisions on the universe, God or genetics. The moment you do that you become trapped by a self-fulfilling prophecy and you're no better than Doctor Sen.'

Diana threw her arms around her beau, 'I'm sorry Vic.'

He embraced her, 'Do me a favour and don't talk like Joshuyo. If I fuck up I'll take responsibility.'

'I'm afraid I might lose you Vic.'

'Why?'

'She's smarter, better looking, has a better job.'

'If she was so smart she wouldn't have been on the run. As for her job she's a glorified proctologist,' Diana laughed into his chest, 'and you're the most beautiful woman in this universe.'

She looked up at him with doubt in her eyes.

'Go easy on yourself Dee, you've got far more going for you than her, besides I love you, I don't love her.'

They kissed, sealing his comforting words but they were more than mere comfort for it was the truth. Nori was a beautiful woman but he loved Diana, Diana had fought by his side, she'd dragged him from the doldrums on the Charon, established the path he was to walk, she'd reminded him of his obligations when poor and needy suffered, she was the light which guided his soul as a torch illuminating the innards of a cave, even if he didn't know it, she was his salvation.

## The End

www.ingramcontent.com/pod-product-compliance
Lightning Source LLC
Chambersburg PA
CBHW070505130626
46555CB00003B/1161